The
Family Greene

The
Family Greene

a novel by
Ann Rinaldi

Harcourt
Houghton Mifflin Harcourt
Boston   New York   2010

Harcourt is an imprint of the Houghton Mifflin Harcourt Publishing Company.

www.hmhbooks.com

Library of Congress Cataloging-in-Publication Data
Rinaldi, Ann.
The family Greene : a novel / by Ann Rinaldi.
p. cm.
Summary: Follows Caty and her daughter Cornelia through the latter half of the eighteenth century as they mingle with the heroes of the Revolutionary War, discovering that a woman's only means of power, flirting, can cause trouble and confusion.
Includes bibliographical references.
ISBN 978-0-547-26067-9 (hardcover : alk. paper) 1. United States—History—Revolution, 1775-1783—Juvenile fiction. 2. Greene, Catharine Littlefield—Juvenile fiction. [1. United States—History—Revolution, 1775-1783—Fiction. 2. Greene, Catharine Littlefield—Fiction. 3. Sex role—Fiction. 4. Mothers and daughters—Fiction. 5. Washington, George, 1732-1799—Fiction. 6. Wayne, Anthony, 1745-1796—Fiction.] I. Title. PZ7.R459Fam 2010 [Fic]—dc22
2009049967

Text set in Adobe Garamond.

Manufactured in the United States of America
DOC 10 9 8 7 6 5 4 3 2 1
4500218155

The Family Greene is a work of fiction based on historical figures and events. Some details have been altered to enhance the story.

For my son, Ron

Who played the role of General Nathanael Greene for so many years in the Christmas Day Crossing of the Delaware, before he played George Washington. Who loaned me the right books from his extensive library on American history for research, cautioned me against the wrong books, and inspired me to write historical novels in the first place, and . . . for always being there.

PART ONE

Caty Littlefield Greene

May 1764
Block Island
Twelve miles off the Rhode Island coast

THE SEA was still angry, showing its anger with its white foam spitting at all comers.

Caty admired it as she stood there on the ruined beach. It was just the way she wished she could be sometimes, if she hadn't been doomed to be a lady.

It was a noisy sea, too, something she wasn't allowed to be, which was why she admired it so much more than when it was quiet. And now, after the storm, it was strewn with the wreckage of a ship. Broken masts and spars, pieces of bunks, the captain's own spyglass floating about, baskets of fruit, and, on a crossbeam, a black cat sitting there meowing out its distress.

"Oh, you poor kitty," she said, and without thinking, or taking off her shoes, Catharine Littlefield, all of ten years old in this year of 1764 and always willing to take charge of things, waded in, sloshing about in the warmish water amid splinters of wood, colored stones at her feet, and the bright green moss that usually clung to the pilings that stood in the normally clear water. She picked up the cat.

"What are you going to do with her?" her friend Sarah, standing by at the shore, asked.

"Take her home," Caty answered.

"I thought you weren't going home today."

Caty paused for just a second. "I suppose I have to go home sooner or later. Though," she added, "if not for Pa, I'd just as soon wait here for the next pirate ship that comes by and go with them wherever they're going. I'd even help them look for my great-grandfather's trunk full of gold."

"Caty, you're so full of fantasy, you sometimes don't know the truth."

"It'd help *you* to have some fantasy in your head."

The cat purred and nestled against her. She stroked it and wrapped her shawl around it. She looked about. Some of her elders who lived on Block Island had already been to the beach this morning and rescued any survivors.

Now, except for two curious women in riding breeches who lingered (all the women on the island rode astride, to the horror of visitors from the mainland), there was no one about. Caty and Sarah had already bade these two women good morning. They were Mrs. Garfield and Mrs. Heron, sisters who had both lost their husbands and now occupied the old Warren house near the meeting hall on the island.

Once again Caty looked down at the spyglass floating near her. "Here, take Puss," she directed Sarah, who did. And so she reached out and grasped the spyglass. "For Pa," she told her friend. And this, too, she wiped dry on her shawl.

Then she reached again for the cat, and with it and the spyglass in her arms, she stepped out of the water while Sarah went sloshing about in it.

For a moment Caty turned to enjoy the view of the island, Block Island, with its rows of stone fences and its rough terrain. She knew every tree, every path, every twist and turn of it. Her eyes caught the straight lines of the houses drawn against the now bright blue May morning sky, the New England houses standing unafraid before all the winds and storms. More than fifty houses!

Imagine! Imagine what the island had looked like in 1600 when the colony of Massachusetts Bay "acquired" it from the Indians. Though she'd never been to school, Caty knew all about the history of the place. Wasn't she helping her father to write a book about it?

The island was then sold to a private syndicate and eventually ended up in the hands of Simon Ray, Caty's great-grandfather.

Twelve miles off the Rhode Island coast, belonging to Rhode Island now. See? I know my lessons. Who says I need a tutor?

This is my world, she told herself. *And that's why I don't want to leave it.*

CHAPTER ONE

GRIMES, OUR HIRED man, was up on the hill, waving a handkerchief at Sarah and me, which meant that I must go in for breakfast.

"I don't want to go in," I told Sarah.

"But it's your birthday. You must go," Sarah insisted.

I was ten years old today. Pa was making a big fuss. That thought alone quickened my senses. Aunt Catharine had arrived late last night on a double ender from the mainland just before the storm hit. I'd been abed when she came, and kissed her hello in the dark, half asleep.

A double ender was a sailing vessel for which our island was famous. It could be launched from beaches and was equipped for both sailing and rowing. Its masts could bend in the wind without snapping. And few places on the northern coast had winds as sharp as we had.

I looked at Sarah. "Are you coming to breakfast with me? You know you're invited."

She looked down at herself. "I'm wet and filthy."

"You've looked worse for wear at our table."

"To what end? You know why your aunt Catharine is here today."

"To take me to East Greenwich to live with her, because she says I need tutoring. But I won't always stay there."

"Once you go you won't come back. She'll make you a fancy lady, like she is," Sarah said sadly.

Aunt Catharine, my mother's sister, was a lady of quality, with mannerisms that matched her beautiful face. The word *pretty* did an injustice to her dark hair and hazel eyes. My mother, who had died only six months ago, had been beautiful, too, but she had not had hazel eyes.

Aunt Catharine had always fascinated me because there seemed to be some mystery about her I could not get a purchase on.

"It's just for tutoring," I told Sarah now.

"Well," she admitted, "none of us has really been to school."

"Nothing wrong with how I speak. I can read and do sums."

"But your pa says your spelling is most crude," she insisted.

"Well, so is yours."

"But I'm not being given the chance to have a tutor."

"You want one?"

Sarah shrugged. "I want more for you to be here with me and help me find your great-grandfather's gold. Everybody says it's buried somewhere in these cliffs."

"You can keep looking while I'm gone. Just don't fall down the cliffs."

"I know." Sarah smiled her sweet smile. "You had better go, Caty. The fish and eggs are likely to get cold."

Always the voice of reason, I thought of my friend. *How I shall miss her when I go to the mainland!*

We walked up the cliff. I hugged the cat and the spyglass, and Sarah held fast to a birdcage she had found. But there was no bird in it.

It's like we're all walking around with empty birdcages, I thought, *looking for the bird we want to put in them. Some get their bird. Some never do.*

We were in front of my door now and just stood there staring at each other. Of a sudden the door opened.

There was Pa in his velvet morning coat. "Caty, child, I've been waiting for you." He gave a little bow to Sarah and she curtsied to him. "How are you this morning, Sarah Cogswell?"

"Fine, sir."

"Will you come in and sit at table with us?"

"I wouldn't make good company, sir. My mum needs me. She and my pa are at loggerheads again."

Pa nodded but said no more. He just stood there, puffing on his pipe, the smoke rising white against the blue sky. He knew that Sarah had troubles at home, that her mother often "took up" with other men, mostly sailors who came to the island. Except for me, Sarah kept mostly to herself. Most people on the island knew about her mother's transgressions, and the shame was just too much for her to abide.

On one or two occasions, Mrs. Cogswell had disappeared for a day or two with her sailor, off to the mainland. At those times, Sarah "kept home" for her pa, cooking and cleaning for him. Times like these I asked Pa if I could take over a platter of chicken or a tureen of soup and he'd always said yes, but with the maxim "Be careful it doesn't look like charity."

Mrs. Cogswell always came home, but I knew Sarah never forgave her.

Now Pa patted Sarah's shoulder. "You're welcome whenever you want," he said. "Tell your pa that last pair of boots he made me are better than anything I could get on the mainland."

"I will, sir."

Then Pa turned to me. "Well, Prodigal Daughter? Are you ready to come home and face the music?"

He hugged me and I hugged back, the cat between us meowing in my shawl. "What's this?" he asked, pretending sternness. "Puss in Boots?"

"I found her in the wreck, Pa. I couldn't leave her. So I brought her home. Please, can I keep her? We haven't had a cat since Simon died."

"I'll keep her for you. She'll be company when you're away." His mischievous blue eyes begged me not to cry, so I didn't. He heartily approved of Aunt Catharine's plan to take me to the mainland. "You think I want the prettiest girl on the island to be uneducated?" he'd asked.

We went inside. Pa sat down at the head of the table and gestured I should sit at his right, where he'd saved me a place. I did so, putting my shawl and the spyglass on the floor at my feet.

The cat was in my lap. Pa put a piece of fish on a small

dish and handed it to me. "Put it on the hearth and give it to Puss in Boots as a welcoming present," he said.

I got up, kissed him, turned, and bumped into Aunt Catharine.

"Good morning, Caty," she said. "And happy birthday."

I set the plate down for Puss, then gave Aunt Catharine a proper hug and kiss, which meant being enveloped in her silk clothing and, for the moment, being carried away in the mystery of her, of far-off places and mysterious doings that the sensation of her always gave me.

What does it all mean? I wondered.

"You must sit down and eat," she admonished. "Don't rush. I'm staying the day, until the winds die down. It ought to be a calmer trip back. I know how you hate sailing in rough weather."

"Aunt Catharine, I want to go with you, but oh, I hate to leave home and Pa."

"You're growing up, Caty. You are becoming a beautiful girl. There will be a need for you to correspond, soon, with young men. You can't even spell, child. And you come from a family of eminence. We want you to marry well. An education is a great part of it."

There it was in a nutshell, then. I was ten years old and they were thinking of my marriage someday. "I'll eat now," I promised. "But first I have a gift for Pa."

HE LOVED THE SPYGLASS. He pronounced it "first rate." And before the noon meal, Puss in Boots was on his lap and he was settled in his stuffed chair in front of the big bow window that looked out over the farmland, down to the sea. My cousin Sammy Ward, who was two years younger than I and interested in whether there had been any dead bodies on the beach this morning, sat at Pa's feet with me as Pa told us stories.

The stories were interrupted all morning by the comings and goings of people stopping in to bring me presents, more out of respect for Pa than to honor me. For presents I got books, gloves, a new apron, a dress made for me by Aunt Catharine herself, and a hand-drawn map of the island and a bracelet made out of seashells from Sammy.

The fragrance of Cassandra's special vegetable soup and fresh biscuits drifted in from the kitchen. It was just then that there came another knock on the door and Sammy got up to open it and admit Mr. Tosh, who tended his fishery for a living and whose ancestors had been sold to English colonists in the New World by Parliament after being captured by Cromwell at the Battle of Worcester.

Mr. Tosh fancied himself and his forebears my mother's ancestors. Thus he always considered it a right—no, a duty—to periodically have a say in matters that concerned our family.

"Have a toddy, Mr. Tosh, won't you, in honor of my girl's birthday." Pa stood and shook the man's large hand.

Mr. Tosh said nothing. He brought nothing. But he drank what Pa gave him, in one gulp, then put the glass down on the table. "I come, Mr. Littlefield, in the spirit of friendliness, to report to you that your little girl here has been spending too much time with that Sarah Cogswell, whose mother runs loose with other men. Your Caty, sir, is a lovely child, carefully brought up and doing the family proud. I'd like to put in a complaint about her keeping company with that Cogswell family. And that, sir, is why I have come hither."

Silence. My pa wasn't quick to respond. Silence so long this time that I felt I should respond. I said, "Sir."

But that's all I said. For Pa's hand was on my shoulder like a fox's paw on a rabbit. So I shut my mouth and waited.

"Mr. Tosh, after a most delicious bowl of soup made by Cassandra," Pa announced, "Caty and I are going to take a walk outside, just the two of us, before she leaves this evening."

Mr. Tosh seemed to understand.

Sammy said he was going to saddle up and go for a ride. So after our soup and crackers, I wrapped my shawl around myself and Pa changed into his walking clothes and we took the familiar paths on the island that I knew so well.

CHAPTER TWO

"WELL, DAUGHTER," Pa said as we reached the top of the craggy hill and looked down on the meadows, the houses, and the crisscrossing stone fences that lay like a quilt below us. I was glad Pa had chosen this spot. It was the top of the world on Block Island. Come up here and it wasn't hard to think you were in charge of everything.

"Well, daughter, and so you're going away now to school."

"To Aunt Catharine's house," I corrected him.

"It's all the same to me. I feel like a father sending his daughter away to an expensive school. And I think you'll find out that's what Aunt Catharine's place really is. Oh, don't protest. She's doing what is right for you, and I don't know what we'd do without her. But I have to tell you something, nevertheless."

"Yes, Pa."

"The one reason it worries me, sending you away right now, is because in these next few months I intend to take me a new wife."

I blinked up at him. "The Widow Ainslie?" I asked.

He'd been courting her of late. I'd have to be blind as an owl in daylight not to see he was besotted with her.

"Yes, and I don't want you to feel that I'm sending you off to be rid of you because of my intentions to take her to wife."

I went to hug him. My father was, as Aunt Catharine always said, "part of the landed gentry" on the island. I knew that John Littlefield was a man of eminence, a man to be reckoned with, and a man who would never live with a woman without marriage. So it was the natural course of events right now. And if I had to go and live with Aunt Catharine to make life easier for him, I would go.

It would be no easy task leaving him, but he deserved this happiness.

"You wed again anytime you want to, Pa," I told him as we started back down the path. "I don't want you to be lonely."

"Thank you for your blessing, daughter."

The bell on the meetinghouse rang then, six times.

It was time to go. Aunt Catharine had paid the boatman a special price to be at the beach to fetch us at six o'clock if the water becalmed itself.

Cassandra and Aunt Catharine had packed my bags.

Father kissed and hugged me as if I were making the trip across the water only for a visit. Then we went down the path, with Aunt Catharine and Sammy, to the dock, where we would get the double ender.

Pa halted. "Wait. There is one more thing." He took a deep breath and looked around at the lovely landscape as if it were going to disappear. "You're going to East Greenwich, a real town, with gossip and dancing masters and tutors and politicians. You'll hear things you don't hear on Block Island. Like rumors of a coming unrest between the British, who are extracting revenue from us colonists, and us colonists, who are thwarting them."

I scowled and nodded as if I understood.

"Just keep your eyes and ears open and your mouth shut," he said. "And listen to your uncle Greene. He knows what's going on. He's a Rhode Island political leader."

"Yes, Pa," I said.

The breeze was mild. The whitecaps on the water became calmed. Inside my heart, they were angry, tossing, spitting, wrecking everything in sight. And nobody knew it but me.

We continued down the path and waited for the boat.

I heard my name, a whisper carried on the misty evening air. "Caty."

It was Sarah. Oh, how glad I was that she'd come!

"Pa, I must say goodbye to Sarah," I told him. He nodded his permission and I ran over to the form waiting in the distance. I hugged her. "Oh, I wanted you to come for supper."

"Ma was only middling well. I wanted to stay with her. Here, I have a present for you." And she handed me a small book-size package wrapped in brown burlap. "It's a diary. So you can keep the days. And so you won't forget to tell me everything."

"Remember, you promised to come and see me."

"I will, I will. Mayhap I'll come with Ma someday."

"Good. You do that. Is there something you wanted to tell me, Sarah?"

There was. I could tell by her hesitant manner.

She dug into the stones at her feet with her shoe. "Yes. Your aunt Catharine. Did you know she had a romance?"

"She's married. To Uncle Greene."

Sarah nodded. "A woman can have a romance when she is married."

I just stared at her. There was something meaningful in her eyes. And it connected with me. So *that* was the mystery I suspected about Aunt Catharine!

"Who with?" I asked. "And is it still going on?" My breath was caught and taken by the wind.

"Benjamin Franklin." The same wind took the name from her lips and carried it away.

I drew in my breath. The wind would not take the name from me. I would hold on to it. Forever. *Benjamin Franklin.* "How do you know?"

"My mother knows a lot of people. She told me. It's what they say. Your aunt Catharine and Benjamin Franklin have been close for years."

I believed Sarah. She didn't mouth off just to hear her own voice. "Ohhh," I said.

"It ought to be interesting, for you to be mindful of," Sarah said. "I just thought I'd tell you. In case he comes to visit. Mayhap he'll bring some of that electricity of his with him."

He's already brought it, I thought.

We both giggled for a moment. Then Aunt Catharine called and I gave Sarah a final hug and ran back to the dock, hugged Pa, and got into the double ender to leave.

From the double ender I waved until I couldn't see them anymore. "I'll be back," I yelled. "I'll be back soon." But somehow I knew I wouldn't be.

CHAPTER THREE

AUNT CATHARINE and Uncle Greene's house was all white and three stories high, with a porch around the front. It lifted my spirits seeing it sitting there on the top of a ridge.

It reminded me of a wedding cake trying not to melt in the sun.

On an opposite slope, beyond a hill to the east, lay the quaint village of East Greenwich.

The first thing Uncle Greene did, after lifting me off the ground and pronouncing I was prettier than ever, was show me the Boston Post Road that passed by a short distance away.

"You and your aunt can go on a shopping trip to Boston," he said. "Or a jaunt to Providence. You will like it here, Caty Littlefield. I promise."

When Uncle Greene made a promise, he meant it. After all, he was a Rhode Island political leader.

He set me back down. "Do you like our house?"

"Yes, sir. It looks like a wedding cake."

He laughed. "Well, mayhap we can marry you from it someday."

"Take her upstairs to her room, please, Effie," Aunt Catharine requested.

Effie was a free black housekeeper. Uncle Greene did not believe in slavery. The same as my father.

But oh, my room!

It was all green and white! Green, my favorite color. How had Aunt Catharine known?

The walls were papered with a green and white design. The drapes bore the same pattern, and thin, pale green curtains hung straight across the windows. The furniture was of as solid a maple as you could find. The bedspreads carried the same green and white signature of the wallpaper and drapes. I remembered Pa reading me a story about a king in England who had his special colors carried by every knight and cavalier and on every horse and person who represented him.

I felt as if I were in a palace. I ran to look out the front window. And there was a honey locust tree spreading its crown, and birches and maples arching over the yard.

THERE WAS COMPANY for dinner that night. As it turned out, they were Master Herbert and Master Mauriette, my two tutors. Master Mauriette was to teach me French, and Master Herbert my sums and spelling and English.

"But I speak English already," I said most rudely.

"You must learn," Master Herbert admonished, "your

grammar and your spelling. We start school next week. In the meantime, why don't you write a nice essay for me about something, so I can see how far you've come."

"About what?" I asked dumbly.

"Anything. Make it a little story."

I looked at Uncle Greene. "Must I?" I asked.

He shrugged. "He's your tutor, so yes, I suppose you must."

I gave a deep sigh. "Yes, sir," I said.

Now that that little matter was settled, the men started talking politics, a subject that I discovered would many times be brought up at Uncle Greene's table, often with a vehemence that grew more and more intense as I grew older.

This evening it was something called the Stamp Act that caused the meat on their plates to go cold and the forks in their hands to wave in consternation. I could not get a purchase on what the Stamp Act was that night, but I did learn that Uncle Greene was the leader of the Rhode Island Whigs and, as such, was leading resistance to the Stamp Act in the area.

And that he was supposed to write to Benjamin Franklin, in London, concerning it. But had, for some reason, put off the writing.

None other than Benjamin Franklin! *Is he putting off writing to him because he knows of his wife's romance with the man? Will they, then, never communicate about this important matter because Uncle Greene is so hurt about Aunt Catharine's "carrying on" with him? Suppose it is not true that they had an affair? I must find out,* I decided. *Somehow, I must find out.*

"Be careful, darling," Aunt Catharine was saying. "They're still watching the house."

Someone is watching the house? Oh, how exciting! *Who?* Why, it is like a romance novel, the likes of which Pa allowed me to read only if I did all my chores.

LATER, WHEN AUNT Catharine came to see me to bed and I asked her who was watching the house, she said, "Nothing for you to worry about."

"Father always told me things. He said I had the most native intelligence he ever saw in a girl my age."

"Well, then, I suppose I shouldn't do any less than John Littlefield did with you. All right. The Tories are watching the house, because we often have men who are staunch Whigs come here to see Uncle Greene to discuss Whig things," she said.

"You mean like the Stamp Act?"

"Yes. People who disagree with the pronouncements of the Crown."

"What do the Tories look like? What do they wear? Any special colors? Do they wear the colors of King George?"

"They dress just like ordinary people, Caty. And they won't harm a girl like you. But I would advise you that if any stranger outside on the street comes up to you and questions you about anything, you should not speak to him. Just come inside the house and tell us. All right?"

"Yes, Aunt Catharine."

I dreamed, that night, about King George III pacing up and down outside our house with dozens of pieces of paper, all stamped and paid for by Colonial money, while inside Uncle Greene sat at his desk and started to write a letter to Benjamin Franklin, then ripped it up and threw it into the fireplace, even though he disagreed with the pronouncements of the Crown.

CHAPTER FOUR

I WROTE THE essay for my tutor. Only it was more of a story, a tale my father had told me one long, cold winter night when I was a child, as I sat in his lap before bedtime.

My father had two uncles, both named Ephraim. The older was a sailor in the British navy and had been lost at sea, so when the second was born, he was named Ephraim in honor of his dead brother. When the second Ephraim grew up, he settled in New England. And one day he met an old man of the same name and who looked a lot like him. As it turned out, it was his brother Ephraim, who was never lost at sea, and so now the family had two brothers named Ephraim.

Master Herbert pronounced that I was a good storyteller but that my spelling was dolorous. He spelled *dolorous* for me. And made me write it. And then he explained the true meaning of it to me.

"Sorrowful, sad, and in pain," he said.

And in the first few weeks of my stay with Aunt Catharine those words began to run through my head every time I looked at Uncle Greene when he did not know I was laying eyes upon him.

Sorrowful, sad, and in pain.

He would be sitting there in the sun in the parlor, before the great windows, pretending to be reading a book but gazing instead at some middle distance and looking sorrowful, sad, and in pain.

Or he would be at his desk in his study, bent over his ledgers, his pen poised in midair. Sorrowful, sad, and in pain.

Or betimes at the supper table, his fork poised with a piece of meat on it, watching Aunt Catharine chatter, looking sorrowful, sad, and in pain.

And I would think, *He believes she is in love with Benjamin Franklin. He thinks she has been carrying on with him. And he has not yet written the letter to Mr. Franklin that he knows he must write. He cannot bring himself to do it.*

I had come to love Uncle Greene in the near month I had resided in his house. He had a quiet, gentle firmness about him. He was a dear man, with a real love of country. A learned, respected, and modest man. And his love for Aunt Catharine was deep and abiding.

Myself, I did not care if she had a romance with Mr. Franklin. Part of me quickened to the thought, was intrigued by it. The other part needed to prove it was untrue, for the sake of Uncle Greene. And I would, somehow, the first chance I got.

My chance came about a month after I arrived at their house, when I sneakily went about searching Aunt Catharine's room. She and Uncle Greene were out for the afternoon, paying calls. The house was empty, quiet, and I'd found Aunt Catharine's old trunk under her bed with letters in it—letters from my mother, from their sister, Judith, in Boston, and finally from Benjamin Franklin himself.

I should have read the ones from my mother. Another time I would have. But I picked up instead a yellowed parchment from Benjamin Franklin, detailing how he and she had tarried several days in Newport before she was married, though he was married and a father. And how they had been so in love.

But there was nothing to indicate that they had been lovers.

When they separated after that trip was over, he still wrote to her. In one letter he complained of her "virgin innocence" on the Newport trip.

I rushed through the letters breathlessly, hoping to find something that would either incriminate Aunt Catharine or free her of the charge. But all I found were references by Franklin of two visits he'd made to this house after Uncle Greene had married her.

Oh, there were constant references to how he loved her, would never forget her, but no words that would link them together as lovers.

I had set the final letter down in my lap and was gazing at a bee that had just flown in the open window and settled on the fold of the drape, not knowing whether to be relieved or disappointed, when I was jolted out of my romantic reverie by Aunt Catharine's voice from the doorway of her room.

"So! Here you are, you little minx! Well, you have some explaining to do! What are you about, going through my personal things?"

I wanted, at that moment, to be that bee, to be able to fly out the window into the blue afternoon. My head whirled. My head hurt of a sudden with the effort of turning to look at her.

"You're not supposed to be home yet," I said stupidly.

"Well, you miscalculated, didn't you? Dishonest people usually do."

Dishonest? She considered me dishonest, then!

She came into the room and across the highly polished hardwood floor and brightly braided rug, throwing aside her shawl and bonnet at the same time as she scooped up the letters that were on my lap and all over the floor.

"Get up," she ordered.

I got up.

"Is this how I can trust you? The minute I leave you alone you search about in my personal things?"

I felt as if she had slapped me. "Aunt Catharine, I'm not dishonest. I'm trying to straighten something out, to bring out the truth about you."

She stood before me, straight and justified. "There is no truth to bring out. Or is it that old saw about me and Mr. Franklin again?" She glanced at the letters in her hands. "These are all from him. Is that it? Who's been feeding you gossip?"

I did not answer for a moment. Then I said, "I cannot betray a confidence."

That seemed to mollify her. "Very well, if you won't tell me who fed you the gossip concerning me and Mr. Franklin, then tell me this. Do you believe it?"

I lifted my chin and looked her full in the face. "No," I answered. "I mean, I think he loves you, Aunt Catharine. But I don't think you did anything wrong. Did you?"

"No," she said. "But if the gossips want to believe it, let them. Go on. There is more. Tell me what is eating at you. I don't think you're the kind of person who would hold it against me if I did carry on with Mr. Franklin. There is too much of me in you, Caty Littlefield. But you came up here to find out for another reason. Now, what is it?"

I sighed and told her then. "Uncle Greene has a sorrow about him. I believe he thinks you did. And I think you should tell him you didn't and take his sorrow away."

She was silent, pensive, for a moment. Then she spoke. "He should trust me. I have been a good wife to him. We have a good marriage. And trust is part of it," she said. "I shouldn't have to tell him something like that."

Then she gathered the letters and put the chest back under the bed. "But you should know this, Caty Littlefield," she said, and she stood, looking at me. "We women always have the right to flirt. *If* it is kept a harmless pastime. Men expect it from us. Done properly, it gives us power, and Lord knows we have little of that. It is even our responsibility as a hostess. But it *must be learned to be done properly.* Do you understand?"

I said yes, I did.

She expected Uncle Greene to trust her. Was that right? No, I concluded. Uncle Greene reminded me too much of Pa for me to allow him to suffer. And if he needed her reassurance in face of the gossip, she should give it to him.

And if she wouldn't, somehow I would.

I AVAILED MYSELF of the opportunity one day a week later. Some important men were coming for supper, and Uncle Greene did what he never did. He went into the kitchen to make sure the table would be set with food in great plenty. He personally set his best wines on the sideboard.

I watched him carefully.

"They will be grim-faced with me tonight, child," he said. "I have not yet written my letter to Mr. Franklin."

We were alone in the dining room. I was allowed to light the candles. As I lighted the last one on the table, I looked across the white cloth at him and summoned all my courage.

"Uncle Greene, may I have a word with you? I have something important to tell you."

It may have been the look on my face. Or the tone of my voice. But he knew something was in the air, something as palpable as the fragrance of the candles I had just lighted. He looked about for a moment, then gestured that I should come with him into the darkened parlor. I followed.

And there, in the midst of shadows and the half-hearted light from the candles in the dining room, which gave flickering hope, I told him about my transgression, my searching of Aunt Catharine's trunk of letters and how she found me and told me she and Mr. Franklin committed no transgression.

I saw his eyes go soft. But he said nothing.

"She said if people want to believe it of her, they can go ahead and gossip," I told him. "I'm telling you, Uncle Greene, in case any of your friends says anything against her. You mustn't let them say it."

"I would never let them say it, child."

"She said she never told you this. I told her she must."

"There is no need, child." He smiled his lie. "Our marriage is based on trust."

Now I smiled my lie. "Of course." Then I hugged him. "How silly of me to think otherwise. Come, we must go back and finish lighting the table."

His friends were grim-faced that night, just as he suspected, and though they ate and drank with gusto and tried to keep the conversation general, Aunt Catharine ordered the coffee in the parlor for them because the noises they made about the Crown were getting louder and louder. Soon the smoke in the parlor got thicker and the conversation got louder, and I heard Uncle Greene say, "Tomorrow I post my letter to Benjamin Franklin," and the doors of the parlor closed.

I went to sleep that night knowing that I had done the right thing.

OUTSIDE ON THE STREET a week later, there was a Tory walking up and down and scolding the Patriots. We were used to him. He came all the time to "watch" Uncle Greene's house.

"Traitors! Whigs!" the Tory was chanting. "There's still time to take the king's shilling and declare your patriotism!"

He had been chanting it for a full five minutes before we inside could make out the sense of it. Aunt Catharine slammed her fist down on the desk. "Isn't there any peace and quiet around here?" Then she got up and swished her skirts away from the desk and went out a side door, slamming it behind her.

A page of a letter flew onto the floor. I rushed to pick it up. And that's when I saw the salutation: "Dear Benjamin."

She was writing to Benjamin Franklin!

I read on. And I read very fast. She was writing to him in London and asking when he would be home. When he came home, he must come to her house for dinner!

She asked after his favorite sister, Jane Mecom, and told him about how I was living with them now. *Please come home soon,* she begged.

I put the page back on the desk. Aunt Catharine was

coming into the house. I quickly went to greet her at the door. "Was he a Tory?" I asked.

"Yes, and the worst of them. The king's shilling, indeed. What does the man think we use now? Gold doubloons?" She gathered up her skirts and sat herself down again in her chair by the desk. "I must finish this letter. Do you think you could post it for me, darling? I do want to get it in the mail today."

I said yes, I could.

JUST AROUND the corner from our house, on my way to posting the letter, I saw him standing there in the middle of the street under the arching trees, looking at me.

"Ah, the little miss who belongs in the big white house. What is your name, little miss?"

"Are you the Tory who's been yelling at us all day?"

"I wouldn't call it yelling, child. I would call it trying to enlighten some poor souls who have lost their way in the middle of all the claptrap that's been circulating around the colonies of late. I would save you from yourselves. Why do you go against your king?"

"I think you should get off our street."

"This is, by rights, the king's highway."

"Well, I don't see him anywhere about, do you?"

"Ah, a feisty little piece, is it? We could use you on our side. What do you say?"

"I didn't know there were sides."

"Come, now. Isn't your uncle the popular Whig known as Greene?"

"He's my uncle Greene, that's all I know."

"And he attracts the Whigs round and about to his abode. To discuss dissension."

"Could you please let me by? I have to post this letter and get home. It'll soon be suppertime."

His eyes had been on the letter in my hand. "You *are* feisty, aren't you?" He was speaking softly now and in a hypnotizing tone. "Aren't you afraid I'll report you to someone important?" All the while he was reaching his hands out. With one, he took my wrist. With the other, he wrested the letter from my hand. "Important correspondence to a Boston Whig, perhaps? Shouldn't it be stamped and taxed by the Crown?"

I tried to resist him, but it was too late. He had the letter. And in no time he had it opened.

"Give that back to me!" I demanded. "It's my Aunt Catharine's private correspondence!"

But he held it above my head, and me at bay while he read it. "Ah, so I see. She corresponds with the most notorious Whig of all. Benjamin Franklin. 'And when are you coming home?' she asks. 'You must come and have dinner with us.' Good to know, little miss. Now we'll really have to keep an eye on your house."

I was crying out of agitation by now. Hating myself. I couldn't even post a letter without failing.

"Don't cry," he told me. "Here, I'll restore the envelope for you." And out of his haversack he took some magical things and resealed the letter so no one would know it had been played with.

He gave it back to me with a mock bow. "Go on your way, with God," he said in a most polite manner.

All kinds of wonderful words wanted to run off my tongue, words I'd learned from my cousin Sammy Ward, but I could only nod and run, terrified by what had just happened.

I had been accosted by a Tory! He had taken a letter of Aunt Catharine's from me and read it, and now he knew Benjamin Franklin was coming!

I ran all the way to post it and all the way home again. When I got there Aunt Catharine knew something was wrong, but I would not tell her. I could not tell her. I just said I'd been chased by a wild dog.

CHAPTER FIVE

I̲N JULY, Benjamin Franklin did come to dinner.
  He and his nineteen-year-old daughter, Sarah, drew
up in a chaise in front of the house. In back of the chaise
a saddle horse was tethered.

Aunt Catharine ran out to meet them. She hugged
Sarah and then, after Mr. Franklin gingerly allowed himself to be helped down by his daughter and Uncle Greene,
she embraced Mr. Franklin, too.

"Easy, my dear." he advised, even as he returned her
embrace. "Easy. I suffered a fall on leaving Mecom relatives in New York. I bruised my chest."

"Oh, my dear." Aunt Catharine drew away, but placed
a hand on his coat front, tenderly. "The poor chest." Then
she kissed the side of his face.

I was embarrassed for her. How *could* she act so? I
looked quickly at Uncle Greene, but he was only smiling.

"And did you not yet invent something to heal it?"
Aunt Catharine asked coyly.

We brought him into the house, into the parlor, where
Aunt Catharine immediately brought coffee for him and
Uncle Greene. She hovered over Mr. Franklin while he
and Uncle Greene launched into a lively discourse about

the Stamp Act, which Mr. Franklin said would be re-pealed soon. "Until they come up with something else," he added.

What I was taken with most was the flirtatious manner that Aunt Catharine used toward him. And so openly! *How can this be?* I asked myself. *Uncle Greene is a good-looking and respected and prominent man. How can she flirt so openly with Benjamin Franklin, in face of all the gossip that has swirled around about them?*

In face of the fact that she herself had never cleared up the matter of the affair which she still thought lived between her and her husband?

The Franklins stayed for a week. In that time, I twice came upon Aunt Catharine and Mr. Franklin alone in the parlor. Once they were sitting together on the settle, heads bent over some papers they had in hand, giggling about something.

Another time Mr. Franklin was seated in a chair and near to dozing and Aunt Catharine came up behind him to wrap a throw around his shoulders in the most tender manner.

He came sharp to attention to look up at her. She smiled lovingly down at him, put her head down near his so their cheeks touched, then their lips brushed and, for a brief second, lingered.

I gasped. Both looked up to see me.

And then, from her position behind him, Aunt Catharine gave me a wink and a small smile. And I recollected her words to me: *Women always have a right to flirt.*

If it is kept a harmless pastime. Done properly, it gives us power.

I ran from the room, my feelings swirling in my head. I admired Aunt Catharine on so many counts. I wanted to be like her in so many ways. But in that place inside you where you know things are wrong but you don't know yet why, and you don't want them to be wrong, I knew that someday I would find that she was lying.

BENJAMIN FRANKLIN'S daughter, Sarah, was a student of the harpsichord, and during their stay she played it constantly. Uncle Greene went to Providence almost every day, and on two days he took the esteemed Mr. Franklin with him, thank heaven. Or Lord knows what might have transpired in our house. Twice Aunt Catharine took me and Sarah on visits to friends.

It soon became plain to me that Sarah adored her father, who often put his arm around her and told her how wonderful her harpsichord playing was. My heart ached for my own father, now happily married to Rebecca Ainslie, who was expecting their first child. Pa was building another family now.

In that week I became morose. My spirits fell low. I scarce spoke at the table.

Of course, Aunt Catharine took notice right off, she who was training me to be a social butterfly. "Caty, what's wrong, child? You're not eating."

It was not the evening to be unsociable. We had other guests, too, some of Uncle Greene's Whig friends.

I looked up at her. I did not answer.

"Caty?" she asked again.

This time I answered. "I miss my pa," I said.

She sighed. "Caty, this is not the way I expect you to behave when we have guests. If you can't behave, you must apologize and go to your room. Now."

One of the Whig friends, a young man named Nathanael Greene, had frequently been a visitor at Uncle Greene's house. I'd never paid mind to him. He was some distant kin to Uncle Greene and had usually been morose in his own right.

My cousin Sammy had told me Nathanael had been totally smitten with Sammy's older sister Nancy, and that she had grown tired of him and severed the romance and broken Nathanael's heart.

I had never known anyone with a broken heart before. I did not know how to speak to anyone with a broken heart. So I had studiously avoided Nathanael Greene, except to notice that he limped. Did that come from a broken heart as well?

Now he spoke up for me.

"I know what it means to miss one's pa," he said, in a rich, mellow voice. "I live with my pa. And I miss him."

What a curious thing to say! Our eyes met across the table.

He had clear, quiet eyes. He was a large man—I had noticed that—at least six feet. He had a firm, no-nonsense face, a mature face. He must have been at least ten years older than I, but there was, somehow, a twinkle in his eye when he looked at me, as if to say "I know all about pas— don't you worry."

Only what he did say to Aunt Catharine, without looking at her, but still looking at me with that twinkle in his eyes, was "Don't make her go to her room, please. She's going to eat. And if she isn't making conversation, well, I'm sure it's because she hasn't got anything to contribute to this tired talk about politics. Isn't that so, Caty?"

I blushed. Just because of the way he was looking at me. No man had ever looked at me that way before. "Yes, sir," I said, "that's so."

"Don't call me 'sir,' please. It makes me feel old. Call me Nathanael. And Mrs. Greene"—he nodded at Aunt Catharine—"Mr. Greene"—he bowed his head at Uncle Greene—"much as I'd hate to miss the lively discussion I know is to follow this scrumptious dinner, I would be delighted if you'd both give me permission to take a walk in the garden later with Caty. I can't help but notice how she's grown up over the time that I've been coming here. I promise to be nothing less than honorable."

HE WAS, in reality, twelve years older than I. And when we sat down on the bench in Aunt Catharine's garden, he fair made me shiver and shake and aware that I was a woman and he was a man.

It was the first time in my life I had ever felt this quickening.

He sat close to me though he could have left space between us. I was well aware of the closeness, but he never touched me, not even my hand. His mere presence was sufficient to put me in a state of terror. To think that this man, this handsome man, wanted to take time to pay mind to *me*.

We talked. He left no spaces, no silences.

He was the son of a Quaker preacher. His mother had died when he was eleven. He was curiosity driven. He loved reading—Locke's *An Essay Concerning Human Understanding*, Ferguson's *Essay on the History of Civil Society*, not to mention Roman history—but he did not lord it over me.

"Why, until a certain age, my only education was the Bible," he said. "I had to beg my pa for a tutor."

"And do you spend most of your time at books, then?" I asked.

"I wrestle iron into anchors. I stoke furnaces. I plow fields. And now, with the help of some of my brothers, I'm building myself a house in Coventry. But I still live in the family home in Potowomut. And I've often seen you, Caty, when you ride your horse by my house."

I stared at him. "You *saw* me? Did you know who I was?"

"Of course. I'd been here in this house to your uncle's meetings many times, though you'd never spoken to me. I thought you didn't like me. Or thought me a pipe-smoking old man who cared nothing about anything but politics."

"You're not an old man. And no, it wasn't that."

"What was it, then? Why did you never so much as give me a glance?"

So he'd noticed! And he'd cared! And here I'd thought all along that he hadn't even known I'd existed. I felt my face flush, knowing I had to say some words, make some sense, or come off like a complete idiot.

"I heard from my cousin Sammy Ward that you had a broken heart. I was afraid to talk to you."

His face went sad of a sudden, but just for a moment. "His sister Nancy. I'm over that now."

"Since when?"

"Since tonight, when I got to know you."

I gulped. What did one say to that? I wished Sarah were here. She'd know. But I found then that I knew, too.

"But you are so much older," I protested. "Why would you even be interested in me?"

"I warn you, Caty, I am. And tonight I intend to ask your uncle if I may begin to come round and see you on a regular basis. We both have time to get to know each other. I can wait. Are you agreeable to that?"

I said I was. Then he said he thought we ought to go back into the house. He must keep his word to my aunt and uncle. For, after all, he had promised to be nothing less than honorable. Could I abide with that, he wanted to know?

I told him yes, I could. He took my arm and guided me back into the house. And his touch thrilled me, even though it was honorable.

CHAPTER SIX

N EVER DID the word *honorable* translate into so much fun for me, and pain, as over the next few years of courtship.

It had taken me a while to get accustomed to the fact that the handsome young man who came a-knocking at Uncle Greene's front door was knocking for me.

Of course, he still came for Whig meetings and I would wait in the parlor, distractedly doing needlework while the meetings went on, praying for them to be over, while Aunt Catharine scolded that I should not appear so anxious.

"Be a little less interested," she would whisper. "Go upstairs to your room. Let him wait for you!"

"Wait for me?" *Is she daft?* "Why should I act disinterested? Don't you remember how it was when you and Uncle Greene were courting? How the minute your eyes met across a room you were together? Couldn't you feel each other's hands? And faces, side by side?"

"And what would you know of faces, side by side?" she would ask. "I hope he is behaving with you. I hope you are behaving as you are supposed to be."

I would sit there and think of Nathanael's broad

shoulders when he took his jacket off, of his strong hands, of the way his face felt when he needed a shave. I would close my eyes and thank God for having made men the way he made them because He, God, had been so clever about it. The way He'd know what we women would want and need.

ONE DAY, Nathanael and I had ridden over to the house he was building in Coventry. It overlooked the Pawtuxet River. Along the river a family was picnicking. Of a sudden we heard a scream from the mother. A little boy had ventured to the edge of the water, fallen in, and was being carried downstream.

In a second Nathanael was off his horse, had torn off his boots and coat, dived in, and brought the boy out. I sat my horse, mesmerized by the sight of him so strong and dripping wet as he handed the boy back to his parents and lingered to make sure the child was all right.

My Nathanael had dove into the river without a thought of his own safety at all! I was besotted with him, and the word *honorable* became more difficult by the day as our courtship went on.

But if it was difficult for me, what was it for Nathanael?

I saw the difficulty for him, as in winter he visited our cozy parlor regularly, as he took me to dances, concerts, fish fries, skating parties. Summertime we went picnicking, sailing, and riding—and more dancing. He was inordinately fond of dancing because when he was young, his Quaker father had never allowed him to dance.

"Once I got beaten because my father was told that I was just *watching* a dance," he told me. So he constantly ran away from home to dance. And was often beaten for it.

But much of the time in our courtship, we gathered in Uncle Greene's house with other Whigs and spoke of the rising rebellion, and many terrible things that happened after the Stamp Act was repealed, like the Boston Massacre in 1770.

By this time, when we said good night, he kissed me, held me close, murmured my name, over and over, then pulled away abruptly. "God," he would say. "God." And I knew it was not an oath, that it was a prayer, as he would turn on his heel and walk away.

It was in that year of 1770 that Nathanael's Quaker minister father died. And upon his death I learned he was not only a minister but a shrewd businessman who owned not only many forges and mills in the area but a merchant ship that was engaged in the Caribbean trade.

The slave trade, Nathanael explained to me.

Of course all of the fruits of his father's industry now went to Nathanael and his seven brothers.

"The merchant ship is called the *Fortune*," he told me, "and we've got to get out of that business soon. But it isn't so easy getting out, once you partake of it. Right now the *Fortune* is carrying fourteen hundred gallons of rum, a hogshead of brown sugar, and forty gallons of Jamaican spirits."

"Who captains the *Fortune*?" I asked.

"Our young cousin Rufus Greene."

"There are Greenes all around me," I accused.

"Yes, dear, and they are all watching how I treat you."

We did not discuss marriage, though the word hung in the air between us, constantly. For, though we were courting, most of the time I did not have him to myself.

It wasn't long before I decided that if I wanted Nathanael Greene at all, I would have to share him with his books, his work, and his politics.

He always had a book in his hand. Heavy reading, I decided, too heavy for me. He read Frederick the Great's *Instructions to His Generals,* for instance. And *An Apology for the True Christian Divinity,* by Robert Barclay.

Right after his father died, Nathanael moved into his own house in Coventry. With permission from Aunt Catharine and Uncle Greene, I helped him move. I assisted with the lighter household things—curtains and pots and dishes—although his brother Jacob's wife, Peggy, was really in charge.

The house, called Spell Hall, was on a small hill overlooking the Pawtuxet River. The first and second floors had four rooms each, with hallways in the center. The third floor was a garret.

In back, overlooking the river, on the first floor, Nathanael had his library. He had at least three hundred books lining the walls.

I could fancy a rainy afternoon with a fire crackling in the hearth, a tray of tea sitting on a low table, and Nathanael sitting at his desk, while I, in that comfortable chair over there, sat reading. What a wonderful way it would be to start a marriage!

Nathanael worked hard most days in the forge that was situated a short distance from the house. He often made miniature anchors, which he sold on his business trips to Newport.

He gave me one. I would treasure it always.

In his "spare" time, he worked in the fields surrounding his house, planting wheat and corn for the animals.

IN FEBRUARY OF '72, the *Gaspee,* a royal schooner that patrolled the waters off Rhode Island to make sure the Revenue Acts were enforced, seized the Greene brothers' merchant ship, knocked about young Rufus Greene, and towed the *Fortune* into Newport Harbor.

Nathanael would not abide this. He brought a lawsuit against Lieutenant William Dudingston, commander of the *Gaspee,* won the case, and became a hero all over Rhode Island.

On the ninth of June, the *Gaspee* was going about its business again when its upstart captain, Dudingston, fired a shot across the bow of an American ship, the *Hannah.* Captain Benjamin Lindsay of the American merchant ship outraced him and led the *Gaspee* aground into shallow waters at Namquit Point, just below the town of Pawtuxet.

I was with Nathanael, Uncle Greene, Aunt Catharine,

and other leading citizens in the Green Grapes Tavern that very night in Pawtuxet, taking a supper of fish and chips, when the news came about the *Gaspee* being run aground after what it had done.

Immediately the group of enraged citizens urged Nathanael to row out and destroy her. I could see Nathanael wanted to. I could see them all plotting over their glasses of ale.

Two other women, sweethearts of two men in the group, were planning on joining them.

I had long since decided that when next I saw my chance, I would be part of what Nathanael was about. I wanted to be included in what he did. And I knew I might never again get the chance.

"Can I go, Nathanael?" I begged. "Oh, please, can I go?"

"You ought to be asking your aunt and uncle that," he said. "Not me."

"Uncle Greene?" I looked at him appealingly.

"She can come with us," said one of the women. "We're going in a rowboat. We'll take care of her."

Uncle Greene said something then that I shall ever be grateful to him for. He looked at Nathanael. "If you two were wed, would you allow her to go?" he asked.

Nathanael appeared taken aback for a moment. But just for a moment. His eyes met Uncle Greene's directly, in solemn understanding. And then he gave a small nod. "Only if she stays with the women. And away from us," he pronounced.

It was done. But what? What was done? Uncle Greene and Nathanael knew. And then, as Nathanael rose and put his hand on my head and left the table, so then, finally, did I.

Whatever happened this night, Uncle Greene had given his blessing for me and Nathanael to be wed. He had turned me over to the care of Nathanael, there and then, over a dish of fish and chips in the Green Grapes Tavern.

SILENTLY, AS figures in a dream, I and the girl named Sally and the other, named Judith, rowed quietly across the waters a good distance from the men. I heard the voice of one of Nathanael's men carry toward us, as voices will carry on the water. "There are scarce more than three or four manning her." Next thing you know, Nathanael and his men were scrambling aboard the *Gaspee*. There was some scuffling in the night. We heard some thuds, some curses, and then a shot, and a man screamed.

"Nathanael!" I started to cry out, but Judith put her hand over my mouth and muffled the sound. Then all went silent. In the next moment, we saw the outline of three men being escorted into our men's boats and then a giant blaze, which grew bigger and bigger in the night, as the *Gaspee* was set afire. We girls sat entranced by the flames that ate up the darkness around us.

"What'll we do with 'em?" a man's voice called out.

"Put them in one of the ship's rowboats," Nathanael's voice answered.

"Lieutenant Dudingston is badly wounded, sir."

"He'll make it back," Nathanael insisted.

Somebody gave the boat with the Englishmen in it a push toward shore, and in the light from the burning ship, I could see the lieutenant seated and bending over in pain. What I did not see was Nathanael's rowboat, with three other men in it, row up beside ours.

"Oh, Nathanael, I'm so glad you're all of a piece."

He handed his oars to one of the men in the boat, who happened to be his brother Jacob. "Take it back to shore," he directed. Then to Judith, "Is there room for me in there?"

All agreed there was. And he hopped into our rowboat and put his arm around me. And I was not at all cold on the way back to shore.

The next day the two of us took a double ender and visited Pa and his wife and family on Block Island. Nathanael was alone with Pa awhile in Pa's study. I petted the cat. I held the new baby. Nathanael had a private talk with Pa. Exactly what was said, I do not know, but when we left, Pa kissed me and said, "If you wish to wed that young man, you have my permission."

Lieutenant William Dudingston of the *Gaspee* had been critically wounded in the escapade that night, and the Loyalists had raised a hue and a cry.

For the first time in the delinquent American colonies, British blood had been spilled. Nathanael was accused, and it struck fear in my heart, but then, with all of New England talking about the incident, Nathanael's name was on everybody's lips again.

He joined the Kentish Guards, a group of fifty-four men around East Greenwich who received a charter from the General Assembly to form a local militia. Nathanael ran for lieutenant, but when the votes were counted, he found that he had lost. His friend James Varnum, a lawyer, became head of the Kentish Guards. Nathanael became morose and thought he had lost because he was a Quaker and had never fired a gun.

Then he thought it was because he had a limp, a stiffness in one knee that he'd acquired from working in the forge.

He wanted to quit the Kentish Guards before he even started. "The uniform is ostentatious," he told me.

It boasted a red coat with green facings, white pantaloons and white vest, silver jacket buttons, knee garters.

He was going to resign, but then his friend Varnum talked him out of it, reminding him how he was needed. He not only stayed on but secured a British deserter to work as a drill master for them. Nathanael drilled with the Guards three nights a week and he pledged his financial support.

All as a lowly private. That was my Nathanael.

I spent many a golden afternoon that fall watching

them drill as the trees shed their leaves in the crisp autumn air. Under the British deserter, they were well trained.

No sooner was one crisis solved, however, than another one cropped up to take Nathanael's attention from me.

Now it was the tax on tea.

What could we do to help the people in Boston who'd had their harbor closed by the British Parliament?

In December 1773 things had gotten even more serious with the advent of the colonists throwing the tea off the ships into the water at Griffin's Wharf in what has come to be known as the Boston Tea Party.

My Nathanael went from being a lowly private in the Kentish Guards to a member of the Legislative Committee charged with the responsibility of preparing Rhode Island's defenses.

Then the General Assembly needed an officer to lead its "army of observation."

Somehow that marked a crossroads in our relationship.

"It's time we married," he said to me one day as we were taking a walk behind his house, looking at the river.

I stopped dead in my tracks. I just stared at him.

"Well, what's wrong? Don't you want to marry me?"

"Nathanael Greene," I said. "It's past time. You've been torturing me for years!"

"Caty, a woman is not supposed to say things like that!"

"Well, I'm saying it! Because it's true!"

"Talk about torture! What about what I've been through! This business of being honorable has driven me mad!"

We embraced. "But you've been so good about it," I told him. "I love you for it. I've watched you suffer and I've loved you for it. You are a dear, good man, Nathanael Greene. You gave me time to grow up."

He rested his chin on top of my head. "You will marry me, then?"

"Try and stop me."

More kissing, then he said, "No more will I have to say a prayer and turn away and say good night. No more."

AND SO we were married soon after, from the wedding-cake house of Uncle Greene's. My friend Sarah was my maid of honor. Sammy Ward was Nathanael's best man. Nathanael's brothers and their wives, my family, and Aunt Catharine and Uncle Greene all gathered around us and wished us the very best of everything to come.

To come was the war. I didn't really believe it then, though I sensed the men did. Surely Mother England would stop her nonsense, with all those ridiculous taxes, and reopen Boston Harbor and go home and leave us be. I wouldn't have believed it if Nathanael told me Mother England would not let us be.

All I knew was that no matter what happened, I would be safe in Nathanael's arms.

CHAPTER SEVEN

W E WERE WED only a short time, and I was sitting in the study, while our cook, Amanda, was cooking a chicken in the kitchen. Nathanael was reading the *Providence Gazette,* delivered weekly by an express rider. I was reading Shakespeare's *Henry VIII,* attempting to find out what these English people were all about.

At the sound of approaching hoofbeats, Nathanael looked across the room at me. "You'd best tell Amanda to set another place at the table."

I started to get up, but he put up a hand to stop me. "No, wait." For the hoofbeats had come to a halt and there was now a pounding on the front door.

"Coming!" Nathanael shouted. And he disappeared into the hall. I set down my Shakespeare, knowing somehow the time for the Bard was long past. And that another time was upon us.

Nathanael did not come back from the hall. I listened to the voices, his and the other man's. They were anxious voices, Nathanael's questioning at first, then concerned. The other man's hurried.

"Can I offer you a rum?" Nathanael said.

"No, I must be on my way. There are others to tell."

"God go with you," Nathanael said, he who wasn't much for God, after being kicked out of Quaker Meeting.

He looked around then, as if to gather himself in. I went into the hall, carrying his cloak and his pistol, his hat and his gloves. "You'll need these, Nathanael," I said.

He then opened the door and called for Britain, a bay stallion, the fastest horse he owned.

In five minutes, while he readied himself, he told me what was afoot. On this beautiful spring day of April nineteenth, news had come to Providence from Massachusetts that British regulars had marched out of Boston to destroy military stores at Concord.

But they were stopped on the Lexington Green by the local militia, men and boys. There were shots. Nobody knew who fired first. All was confusion. But when the smoke cleared, men lay dead on the Lexington Green. And the British regulars marched in the direction of Concord while Americans lined the way, hiding behind trees along the route and firing at them.

There was nothing for it. The war had started.

"I'll be back as soon as I can." Nathanael hugged me.

How many husbands, I wondered, were saying the same thing to wives in Rhode Island this evening as they took muskets down from over fireplaces and mounted restless horses?

I did not cry. I said, "I'll be here."

Nathanael said something about sending Jacob and

his wife, Peggy, over to "see to me," and before I could object he disappeared into the misty dusk of a now damp evening of that memorable day of the nineteenth of April, 1775.

NATHANAEL WENT with the local militia group to the Massachusetts border, where they were stopped by an order from the Tory governor Joseph Wanton. All returned home but Nathanael and two other men, who went on into Massachusetts, where they found that the British regulars, beaten and decimated by the American militia, had retreated to Boston.

So in two days he came home again.

By the time he had returned, I knew a truth that I had only suspected when he first left.

I knew I was with child. Oh, I was so anxious to tell Nathanael! He had wanted a child so badly! But I could not tell him. I knew I could not burden him with such knowledge when he was going off to war again.

"The New England provincial brigades are meeting at Cambridge, Massachusetts," he told me, when home only a few days, "and they're being joined by brigades from middle and southern states. We have to drive the British out of Boston."

Jacob and Peggy came two days before Nathanael left for Cambridge. I liked Jacob. He was easygoing and paternal, a little like Uncle Greene. But Peggy proved to be as she had been when I helped Nathanael move into his house: sharp around the edges and immediately wanting to establish her superiority over me.

And she did so in those two days in the only way she could. In a way that left me in tears and acting like a little girl in front of Nathanael before he left.

I had taken to throwing up in the mornings because of my condition. Bless Nathanael. He was totally ignorant of the ways of women during their confinement time.

"You must have eaten something strange," he said to me the first morning I threw up into the chamber pot in our room.

Peggy, of course, with her eagle's eye, knew from the moment she laid eyes upon me that I was in a "child-carrying" way.

That first day, she pulled me aside. "How far gone are you?" she asked.

And, "Have you told him yet?"

And, "You mean you're not going to tell him before he goes away? Well, he has a right to know! Don't you think? Now, you tell him today. Or I'll tell him tomorrow!"

She wouldn't, I decided. She wouldn't dare interfere with our marriage like that. And every time I looked at her that first day, she returned the look with a significant one of her own.

And so the second day, after I had thrown up into the chamber pot in our room and was presentable again, Nathanael and I went to the breakfast table as if nothing had happened.

But he said something to Peggy almost immediately. "You'll have to keep an eye on my wife," he told her. "She's not feeling well. She's been having an upset stomach of late."

Peggy's fork clattered to her plate. Her eyes went wide. I clenched my fists in my lap. "You mean she hasn't told you, Brother Nathanael?"

Nathanael was taken aback. "Told me what?"

"I told her if she didn't tell you today, that I would. She's with child!"

Now it was Nathanael's turn to be taken aback. He set his mug down carefully and looked at me. "Caty?" he said. "Is it true? Are you with child?"

I looked up at him and nodded. Tears came to my eyes.

"And you didn't tell me, love? Someone else had to tell me?"

I was blinded with tears, as in a snowstorm. I reached for him in my blindness and he put his arms around me and held me. "I'm sorry," I said. "I didn't want you going off to war and worrying about me."

He rested his chin on top of my head. "My little Caty, going to be a mother. Come." And he pushed back his chair and lifted me up out of mine, and he took me off, through the hall, and into our own room, which was across the way. And Peggy followed, scolding us both the whole while.

"Well, you'd better scold her good. And if I'm to take care of her, you'd better tell her she's to mind me. Do you hear me, Brother Nathanael?"

Without taking his arms from me, Nathanael closed the door of our room with his booted foot.

CHAPTER EIGHT

WITHIN DAYS, Rhode Island's General Assembly called an emergency session. They voted to form a Rhode Island army of fifteen hundred men. And they needed a general to lead it.

They did not pick the natural choice, General Simeon Potter, who was a veteran of the French and Indian War.

They did not pick James Varnum, captain of the Kentish Guards.

They picked a lowly private in the Kentish Guards, Private Nathanael Greene.

Why me? Nathanael wrote to me from Cambridge.

Because, I wrote back, *they know a good man when they see one. Because you are intelligent and you study books. Because you have been reading military tactics for how long now in the bookstore of Henry Knox in Boston. Do you think they do not know this? Because you were the head of a hundred workers at the forge.*

My husband had gone from being a private to being a brigadier general in a few weeks.

I KNEW WITHIN days of his leaving that I could not bear to stay in our house in Coventry with Jacob and Peggy. Jacob was all right, but he spent all his time overseeing the running of Nathanael's forge next door, something Nathanael would be doing if he were home. It was Peggy who was the sister-in-law from hell.

She took over the household the first day she was there.

"Here, let me do that for you—why don't you sit down and rest" became her battle cry.

I did not want to sit down and rest. It was my house. I knew what time the dogs should be fed, that the cats didn't eat what they brought in but only caught it and left their catch to be admired and praised, then must be fed, too, how much the chickens should be given to eat, and yes, that we let the chickens roam free . . . so that I was the only one who knew where they were likely to lay their eggs. Nathanael had shown me.

Peggy thought we were two children playing at house. She quickly "straightened things out."

Within two weeks, the chickens stopped laying their eggs. The dogs stopped eating. The cats stopped bringing in mice.

"What chaos," Peggy said. "How can you run a farm like this?"

Amanda, the cook, quit, and instead of being horrified, Peggy seemed pleased.

"Now," she said with smug satisfaction, "I can teach you to make all the dishes your husband and mine like best."

I had no intention of learning. There was nothing I would hate worse, I knew, than having bossy Peggy standing over me telling me the right way to slice carrots to put in Nathanael's possum stew. Besides, I hated possum stew. I would suffer it if Nathanael were here, but otherwise I'd likely throw up making it.

At home, Aunt Catharine never had time to teach me anything to do with the domestic arts. I led the life of a lady, and the most I'd had to do was learn to stitch a pillowcase or embroider a sampler to be framed and put on the wall.

Besides, in his last letter to me, sensing my unhappiness, Nathanael had written: *I have recommended you to their care, unless they should so far forget their affection for me as to request anything unworthy of you to comply with. In that case, maintain your independence until I return, and if Providence allows I will see justice done you.*

Independence, it seemed, was Nathanael's middle name. I knew he had an excellent rapport with Amanda and loved her cooking. I was sure he would be less than pleased with Peggy to learn that Amanda had quit because of Peggy's troublesome ways.

I decided to make a shopping trip to Providence to settle my mind about things. Mayhap all I needed was a day away from this place, the sights and sounds of different people and scenes. The hustle and bustle of Providence to make me feel part of something again.

I had great sport that day buying dresses that would cover my growing middle. And then, at midafternoon, who did I run into in front of the Cake 'n' Chat, the ladies' tearoom, but Charlotte Varnum, wife of Colonel James Varnum, he who had been captain of the Kentish Guards and friend of Nathanael's and was presently a colonel in the army. He, too, was now in Cambridge.

"Caty Greene!" she cried out on seeing me.

"Charlotte Varnum!" We hugged warmly.

"What in the name of Caesar's ghost are you doing alone on the streets of Providence?" She looked down at my figure. "Why, you're expecting!"

"I had to get away from home," I blurted out. "Nathanael's sister-in-law is driving me mad. Nathanael left her and his brother Jacob in charge. Today she wanted to teach me how to make possum stew!"

"Oh, that's right, my husband wrote me. Nathanael is at Cambridge with the newly formed army. My dear"—she put a hand to her mouth to shield her words—"don't breathe a word of it to anyone until it is made public, but my husband wrote that the head of the whole army is going to be Mr. George Washington from Virginia."

I gasped. "A Virginian? The Continental Congress would never pick a Virginian! Nobody will ever listen to him!"

"What better way to bring this country together?" she asked. "That's what my husband says. Now why don't you and I go inside and have some cake and tea. There are so many things we both need to catch up on."

There are some times in the life of a woman that only

another woman can put reasoning and understanding on a certain situation in her life.

We had tea and cakes. Neither one of us would have ventured in alone. It wouldn't have looked right. Ladies did not take tea alone.

We asked after family at first, of course. We boasted about our husbands, since neither of us had become acquainted, up until then, with the maiming and death this war would bring. Until then it was all military training and practice, music and color.

Finally she said, "Your spirit has been brought low, Caty Greene. Is this because you are carrying? Or because of the gloomy people you are made to associate with? You were always so lively in your aunt's house, so witty and bright. Do you miss Nathanael so?"

"It's all the pieces of a quilt," I said.

She took a deep breath. "Then I think I have a solution for you."

"Short of throwing myself in the Pawtuxet River?" I teased.

"Don't even speak such. Just listen." And she leaned back in her chair and looked at me. "James says that many officers' wives are talking of joining their husbands at headquarters."

What was she saying? That I, wife of a brigadier general, should not stay confined in a house and allow myself to be tortured and brought low in spirit by my sister-in-law when I could go and join my husband at his headquarters near Cambridge?

My heart beat faster. I could be with Nathanael!

"They say that even Mrs. Washington is planning on coming to camp."

"Won't Nathanael object?"

"I'd like to see one man object to having his wife join him. Especially one as pretty as you!"

I blushed, then nodded. "I'll write to Nathanael," I said. "I'll give him some warning, anyway."

I hugged her and thanked her, then, after parting, I told my driver to hurry home. And as we did so that warm July day, I planned, with all the spite in me, how I would act with Peggy, and how I would take no more of her terrible treatment. I was, after all, the wife of a brigadier general, was I not? And I would be treated accordingly from here on in. And it would commence with not having possum stew for supper.

I got home to find the post had come and there was a letter from Nathanael, telling me how much he loved me and missed me and wished he could see me. He had moved his headquarters to Prospect Hill, two miles from Cambridge. He wrote that George Washington had been appointed commander in chief of the whole army by the Continental Congress.

I've met him. He's a fine fellow. The kind you want on your side, he wrote. *We can't but be the victors with him in charge . . .*

I wrote back, telling him how I met Charlotte Varnum, how she'd told me that many wives were talking about traveling to Cambridge to be with their husbands. Did he not want me to come?

He wrote back. He said a lot of things—news, gossip, how he could see the enemy's garrisons from where he was. But he never said no, I should not come.

I seized on that. I betook myself to Providence another day. I bought a whole new wardrobe and a trunkful of baby clothes, and when the driver, whose name was Sergeant David Shaw and who was one of Nathanael's Kentish Guards on leave, dropped me off, I bade him pick me up at the house at six the next morning.

"For Providence again, Mrs. Greene?" he asked.

"No, for Cambridge," I answered.

"But that's fifty-two miles, ma'am, a two-day drive. We'll have to make an overnight stop. Change the horses."

"Aren't you up to the task, sergeant? To bring your commander's wife to visit him?"

He snapped to attention, if such can be said of one sitting in the driver's seat of a carriage. "Yes, ma'am. I'll tell my wife, make arrangements. I'll be here to pick up you and your bags at six in the morning!"

"Good. I'll bring a basket of vittles, for we'll surely get hungry along the way."

Begrudgingly, Peggy packed a basket of food, a stone jar of tea, a bottle of wine, biscuits, cold meats, cheese. As she slammed about the kitchen the next morning while Jacob carried my bags to the front door, she, not he, scolded.

"Nathanael will not like this. He'll hold us responsible. And I'll not take the blame for your foolishness."

Jacob took my part, I must say. "She's a grown woman, Peggy. It's up to her to decide. She misses her husband."

Peggy slammed down the stone jar of tea so I thought it would break. "War means sacrifice! Trouble with young people these days is they don't know the meaning of the word."

She went on and on about the failings of young people. The last thing I heard as I went out the door—as Jacob kissed my cheek, helped me into the carriage, and told me to give my best to Nathanael, slipped the driver some extra shillings, and reminded him to avoid the bumps in the road—was Peggy yelling, "And you'll lose the babe on that ride, sure as God made cedar trees!"

CHAPTER NINE

As it turned out, I did not lose the baby along the way.

Sergeant Shaw, on leave because he and his wife had a newborn of their own, avoided the bumps in the road as Jacob had requested. The ride was, indeed, most pleasant. We stopped to take our refreshment. We paused again just to rest, and about five in the evening we stopped for the day. I am not permitted to say where, for the sake of secrecy, because it was at a safehouse halfway to Cambridge, a farmstead owned by Shaw's brother-in-law, a simple saltbox house that had been in the family since 1712.

Shaw's sister and brother-in-law treated me elegantly. They gave us food aplenty for traveling the next day and a fresh team of horses, and shortly after first light, we were on our way.

After the second day of travel, we found the village of Cambridge, surrounded by earthworks. The buildings on Harvard campus were converted into barracks. And where there had heretofore been students, there were now armed soldiers on the streets. Although I had never seen the pretty village of Cambridge before, I felt a pang of loss for what must have been.

But then we got to Nathanael's Prospect Hill Camp. And I saw the stamp of Nathanael's command in the neatness of the soldiers and the precision of their marching routines. More than that, they looked healthy, and I'd heard that they were well fed.

Corned beef and pork, four days a week, Nathanael had written. *Salt fish one day and fresh beef on the other two, with a daily pound of flour, butter, and fresh vegetables.*

As we drew up to the front of Nathanael's headquarters, some troops practicing their drilling across the road came to a halt under directions of a smartly clad officer, raised their muskets in salute, and stood at attention.

The smartly clad officer was, of course, Nathanael. He came over to the carriage and helped me down. As the soldiers had a chance to see I was pregnant, on their own they gave a verbal salute: "Hazzuh, hazzuh, hazzuh!"

Nathanael dismissed them and bent over to kiss me.

"I didn't know you were coming."

"I heard Mrs. Washington was coming, and so I'm here."

"She isn't here yet. Everyone is making ready. And *she* isn't pregnant."

"Are you angry with me?"

"Let's go into the house. Eulinda will make us some tea."

"Who is Eulinda?"

"Her husband is part of the Negro unit we have here. She isn't a slave. She gets paid to help keep my house in order. So she'll be a help to you. How long are you staying?"

"Can Eulinda deliver babies? Are there any women here who can deliver babies?"

"We have doctors," he said.

And then, of a sudden, to show me he was not sorry I came, he lifted me off my feet and carried me into the three-story brick house with the elegant ceiling-to-floor windows and drapes and highly polished wood floors.

He nuzzled his face against mine before setting me down in front of the hearth.

"Eulinda, bring some tea and cakes. This is my wife, Caty," he introduced me.

Her face was young, but her eyes were old and they frightened me. She went out of the room and we heard her shouting some orders, then she came back in.

"Now, why did you make this trip without my permission?" Nathanael asked.

I put my arms around him.

"The baby is due when?" he asked.

"Whenever he chooses to come. He's like his mother."

His voice softened. "What makes you think it's a boy?"

"It is a boy," Eulinda pronounced.

Nathanael hugged me tighter. "Eulinda sometimes knows things," he said. "If only the first one could be. God's stockings, I'd teach him everything I know."

We stood like that, embracing, until a younger version of Eulinda came in with the tea.

"This is her little sister, Patsy," Nathanael said. "She's a treasure. Fetches things that Eulinda won't. Does things, like polishing my boots, that you can't get servants to do anymore."

"That's men's work, Gen'l," Eulinda reminded him. "An' you need a young man around to do such."

"I know," Nathanael said. "Cooper, my last man, went and joined the army. Left me to fend for myself. Patsy, that young man I saw you kissing behind the meat house last night, do you think he'd like a job?"

Patsy grabbed on to a corner of her skirt, gave her older sister a shy look, and said that most likely he would.

"Go ask him, then," Nathanael ordered, and Patsy curtsied and left the room.

I thought, *Why, it isn't much different from a family, the way they speak with each other and giggle. And my Nathanael has made it that way.*

We sat on plain wooden chairs around a Queen Anne's table and partook of our tea and cakes, and I thought, *A boy—mayhap it will be a boy.*

Then came a knock on the door and an aide with a note for Nathanael.

Nathanael read the note, a faint smile on his face. "We are invited to dinner," he said, "given by Moses Brown and his delegation, who have recently come to visit Washington to ask permission to deliver relief to the citizens trapped in Boston, who are running low on food and fuel."

"Why do I know that name, Moses Brown?" I asked.

"Because he was head of the committee that ran me out of the Quaker Meeting in East Greenwich."

"Ohhh." My hand went to my mouth. "And now he invites you to dinner?"

"No, not exactly. He expected to have George Washington at his table. Washington referred him to you and me. He's heard all about your beauty, you see, and your social gifts."

"You jest, Nathanael. Washington isn't even aware of my presence in camp."

"Darling, you had best be apprised of things. Washington knew within minutes of your arrival that you were here. And"—he waved the note in the air, a smile on his face— "he is giving us the honor of appearing in his presence this evening, at nine, after an early dinner with the Quakers."

"Oh! Meet the general! Oh, I must be better dressed! Oh, what shall I do? My hair is all mussed from the trip."

Nathanael smiled, enjoying the moment. He nodded to Eulinda as she came into the room, and with a hand under my elbow, she guided me toward the room that was Nathanael's and mine.

Nathanael followed us into the bedchamber. There, he stood for just a moment. "Caty," he said, "I want you to wear the blue dress. The one with all the ruffles."

I gasped. "But Nathanael, isn't that a bit *daring* to sit at table with Quakers?"

His smile was as the smile of a child who has gotten his own way. "I would say so, yes." Then he turned and started out the door. "Yes, I would say it was a bit daring," he said again. "But I just wanted them to see the beautiful young woman I wed."

CHAPTER TEN

THE TABLE in the dining room of the elegant house assigned to us for the meeting with the Quaker delegation was set in keeping with the American principles and not those of the Quakers. In other words, it was not plain.

The most elegant silverware and crystal sparkled. The finest wine was served, and if the Quakers chose not to drink, so be it. The best cuts of meat were set out by the most well-trained servants.

"Act yourself," Nathanael told me as we entered the house. "Don't try to be something you are not."

Before we sat, both men and women stood around the great fireplace, sipping hot cider. I did my duty and circulated among the plainly clad women, feeling at least like a countess in my blue silk with the scooped neck in front.

"Welcome," I said. "We're glad to have you. I haven't met General Washington yet, but I'm told he's a great man. We're so glad he's on our side."

As formidable a face as that of my hated sister-in-law, Peggy, stared down at me. "That is all fine and dandy, young woman, but does thou know the Lord?"

My mouth fell shut. She was talking about the Lord as if He lived across the street. As if He just moved in and I should bring Him an apple pie.

But I wouldn't be bested. "Yes," I lied.

"Art thou sure thee knows Him sufficiently to some-day dine at His table?"

"He hasn't invited me yet," I wanted to say, sassily. But, of course, I did not. Instead, I said, "Excuse me," and started toward the next group of women. I gave them a greeting much like I'd given the others.

"But does thee know the Lord, child," the eldest said to me. "If not, all this"—and she gave a sweeping gesture that included the table and the whole room—"all this means nothing. And thy General Washington is as nothing."

Well, to insult me was one thing, but to insult General Washington was another. I didn't feel that I had the mettle to defend him. I looked across the room to where Nathanael was standing, talking to a group of men. My look was appealing. *Help me,* it said.

Nathanael recognized only too well that I was in trouble. "Ladies and gentlemen," he announced loudly, "what say we sit at table and eat?"

There was a murmuring of joyous assent. Apparently, the table and all it held did amount to something after all.

It turned out that a smallpox epidemic had broken out in Boston, and Nathanael told our guests he had real fears that it might affect the colonial soldiers surrounding the city.

"You should get yourselves inoculated," he told the Quakers who dined with us.

"The Lord will care for us," Moses Brown said.

"Inoculation near brings on the sickness. It is toying with the work of the Lord," said another. And the subject was dropped.

"You have visited Washington, asking permission to bring relief to the people of Boston with food and fuel," Nathanael told them carefully. "Here is my advice to you. Five years ago you ran me out of your Meeting for having been seen watching a military parade in Connecticut. Now my life is devoted to the military and independence. Now I tell you this. Abide by your own principles, though I have abandoned them. Since you believe in them so much, they will see you through this fight. And though you threw me out of your Meeting years ago, I do not want to see you suffer."

A murmur of approval went through the room for Nathanael, and Moses Brown said he would pray for him.

We parted friends. I stayed close to Nathanael for the rest of the meeting, so none of the women pressed the matter of my knowing the Lord. They seemed afraid of Nathanael. But their eyes went over me in contempt as they left. One or two said they would pray for me, too.

"Do I need praying for?" I asked Nathanael.

"Right now we all do," he said.

I COULD NOT help but be both delighted and afraid for being presented to General Washington.

General Washington! I had always thought that my family was of some eminence in its own right, and I had been trained to be proud of their achievements, but never in all the world did I expect to be in a position in which I would meet someone like General Washington. Or in which my husband would be able to introduce me to him.

"Nathanael," I said, and my voice gave way.

"What is it, love? You aren't frightened of meeting the general, are you? You are." And he hugged me. "You will delight him. Just as you delight me. He loves to have pretty things around him. Oh, and you are not just pretty—you can hold your own, just as you did tonight with the Quakers."

"That's it, Nathanael . . . Did they make me look stupid? I didn't know what to say when they asked me if I knew the Lord."

"Say no, that you haven't been around as long as they have, but that the Lord knows you. Come, smooth your hair. We mustn't keep Washington waiting."

GUARDS STEPPED aside so we could go in to His Excellency's office.

He was a presence. What more can be said of him? General Washington rose from the chair behind his desk in the paneled, book-lined, and map-filled office, and his height was greater than that of any man I'd ever met. His uniform, also, was impressive. Only a few scars from a past case of smallpox marked his face.

As Nathanael introduced me, the general took my hand and kissed it. Then, noting the spread of my dress in front, he congratulated us and asked when the baby was due.

We both answered at once. "Late December."

"Will you go home for the birth or have it here, where we have doctors and you are surrounded by an army for protection?"

We said we didn't know yet.

"My wife has had children," he said. "She comes in early December. When she does, stay close to her. She can advise you."

Then he looked at Nathanael, smiling. "How did you get on with your Quaker friends? Did they invite you back to Meeting?" He was enjoying the joke.

"You set them on me this night," Nathanael accused, "but no, they did not invite me back to Meeting. Only said they would pray for me. Apparently they thought I needed it. But I had their respect. I was in charge of myself."

"You are always in charge of yourself, my boy, which is why you were put in charge of the army of Rhode Island. I would say the General Assembly of Rhode Island made an excellent choice."

Nathanael blushed. "General, may I have your permission to name our babe George Washington Greene if it is a boy?" he asked.

Washington put his arm around Nathanael's shoulder and walked us out of the room. "You may, and I am honored," he said.

CHAPTER ELEVEN

I BECAME a dear friend of Lady Washington's when she came to camp in December, and, in a short time, I became a belle of the camp. We dined frequently at the John Vassal house, where the Washingtons made their home.

There were other guests, of course. The Horatio Gateses, the Thomas Mifflins, he still a Quaker, and most important, General Israel Putnam, near sixty now and a hero of Bunker Hill, and with a scar on his face that bespoke his Indian-fighting days. I begged tales of his escapades from him, and although others had heard them before, they were still intent on listening.

All through this I'd minded General Washington, of course, when he didn't know I was watching him. He'd lean back in his chair and his eyes would sparkle and his face would settle into a small smile as if he himself were remembering his days in the French and Indian War. And he'd sip his wine or his coffee and crack nuts and enjoy himself.

Nathanael and I were invited to every party, every dance. Word got around that I was a "joyous and frolicsome creature," and some of the young aides became downright smitten with me.

"Do you mind," I asked Nathanael, "that people speak of me this way?"

"When I mind, I'll tell you, love. How can anyone mind you, all of nine months with child, joking and smiling and cheering up the homesick men and making them joke and smile. You are the promise of a glorious future to them. You are what they will be fighting for."

And he kissed me.

"Where will I be having the baby?" I asked.

"That is up to you, my girl. Do you want to go home?"

"To what? Your sour-faced sister-in-law? I have friends here in the officers' wives. Might I stay and have the baby here, Nathanael?"

Again he kissed me. "It might be nice someday to tell the young man that he was born in Washington's encampment in Cambridge, while the British guns fired away in Boston."

Just then a shell from a thirteen-inch gun exploded and the very windows rattled. It was, at first, unnerving. And then, on second thought, it was as if God himself had given an answer to my question.

OUR BABY BOY, George Washington Greene, was born in the camp at Cambridge in late December. On the first day of January in 1776, I was up and about for a special event, the unfurling of a new flag of the American union at Cambridge.

Everyone gathered on the parade ground to see thirteen red and white stripes snapping in the wind, with united crosses of St. George and St. Thomas on a dark blue canton. Certainly it could be seen by the British garrisons in Boston and Charlestown as our cannon roared.

In early February, Nathanael was brought low by a sickness the camp doctors named as jaundice.

"I'm as yellow as saffron," he told me from his bed. "I am so weak, I can scarce walk across the room. I am grievously mortified by my confinement, as this is the critical period of the war. Should Boston fall, I intend to be there if I am able to sit on horseback."

"They will have to do without you for now, love," I told him.

But he recovered rapidly, in time to renew his friendship with Colonel Henry Knox, who had just arrived at camp.

Knox was a hero. And we had a party for him. He was the man who'd once been the bookseller in Boston whose shop Nathanael would frequently tarry at to talk of military tactics and, of course, politics.

In a feat of bravado that had people enraptured, Knox had gone on a three-hundred-mile wintertime trip to the captured forts of Crown Point and Ticonderoga, New York. He and his men had traveled over frozen lakes, the Berkshire Mountains, and impossibly high snows to bring back for the American army more than fifty cannon, mortars, and howitzers, and supplies of shells and powder.

Doing all this in late January had been a monumental

task and had made it possible for Washington to fortify Dorchester Heights, surrounding British-occupied Boston. Now Washington's guns towered over Boston, bombarding it. The British would either have to be killed or get out.

At the party, I studied the Knoxes. Henry had recently wed.

He was portly. No, he was downright fat.

And she was as fat as he was. But there was something so sad about her that I immediately felt sorry, and I wound my way through the crowd until I found myself next to her, to start up a conversation.

"Aren't you proud of your husband?" I asked. "He's a hero."

Over a plate piled with food, she looked at me with lovely blue eyes filled, but not overflowing, with tears. *How can she keep the tears from falling?* I wondered. *How does she do that? Oh, if only I could learn to do that!*

"Yes, I'm proud," she said. "But my mother and father are inside the city of Boston, which is even now being bombarded by the guns that my husband brought back for Washington."

For a moment her words made no sense to me. And I had none of my own to respond to them. Only a question, which I knew was intrusive.

"Why are your parents inside the city?"

"Because they are Tories," she answered straightforwardly. "My father is royal secretary to the province of Massachusetts. He never gave his approval to my courtship with Henry, because Henry was a patriot. When we wed, my father disowned me."

"Oh." I minded my own pa and how he'd blessed my union with Nathanael. And I thought, *Why is there always some sorrow attached to the joy and the pride that is given to us?*

Later, when the British evacuated Boston, Lucy Knox told me that her parents had gotten out safely, and she thanked me for my friendship that first night, and for my concern. I had been such a comfort to her, she said.

I had not realized I had been a comfort. What had I done? All I had done was speak to her, listen to her.

I was to remain friends with Lucy Knox most of my life, and as I did not know I helped her, she did not know she helped me that evening.

I learned that once I started speaking to her I never minded at all that she was so fat. I learned that sometimes all you have to do to be a comfort to someone is to speak to them in their moment of anguish, to listen to them.

I learned to control my tears. Anyone, after all, can have tears come to their eyes, but not everyone can keep them from falling over.

It took me a few years, but I learned how to do it. And I am ever grateful to Lucy Knox for showing me the way.

PART TWO

Cornelia

CHAPTER TWELVE

Nathanael Greene's Plantation, 1786
Mulberry Grove
Fourteen miles north of Savannah, Georgia

"CORNELIA? CORNELIA Greene, if you don't come out of hiding this minute and make me stop chasing you like a fool, I'll fetch your father. You hear me?"

Mama was running after me, chasing me. I knew it was not good for her to run seven months into her time, but I also knew that if she caught me, I'd get swatted good and proper. Mama swatted. Pa didn't. And I'd skipped class again this morning. I deserved a swatting.

I hid behind the dry sink in the kitchen. Only my older sister, Martha, who was nine, saw me go behind the dry sink. Would she tell where I was? Likely she would. She was a water snake, Martha was. She never let me forget she was named after Martha Washington, as if a hundred other girls weren't. She was always besting me for Pa's attention and love. She'd even lie to get it. I was always in trouble because I wouldn't lie.

Pa hated liars like he hated "little dirty politicians."

"She's behind the dry sink, Mama!" Martha yelled.

Mama ran into the kitchen after me, then of a sudden there came a thump and a distressed cry. "Oh!"

It was not good. Peeking out from behind the sink, I saw that she fell.

Martha was beside her at once.

I got up from my hiding place and went to her. "Here I am, Mama. Are you all right?"

"How can she be all right?" Martha snapped. "Can't you see? She's bleeding!"

I saw. Blood was seeping out of her, dark and evil, through her dress and onto the floor. She was biting her lip. I knew we couldn't get her up.

"We need help," Martha said. "The servants are never around when you need them. Not even Eulinda." She sounded just like Pa.

But she was right. Old Eulinda, the only paid black servant on the place, who'd been with Mama since the beginning of the war at Cambridge and was usually always at her side, was nowhere to be seen this morning.

"Go and get Pa," Martha said. "I saw him headed toward the coach house."

I ran. Out the back door, down the brick path, past the kitchen garden, and through the yard. Pa was in the coach house, overseeing the brushing of his horse, Tommy.

He looked up as I came in. "Good morning, Cornelia. Where have you been? Mr. Miller said you were not in class this morning."

"Pa, Mama is hurt. She tripped in the kitchen. She's on the floor and she needs you."

The look in his eyes told me he was in the kitchen with Mama already. He brushed right past me and, with long, purposeful strides, walked to the back of the house, giving orders, for there were servants everywhere of a sudden.

"Charles, fetch Dr. Kinney quickly—my wife has trouble. Alice, bring some warm dry blankets to the kitchen and get two other women."

Before going in, he stopped and looked at me. "Where's Eulinda?"

"Don't know, Pa. She's not around."

"How did your mother fall?"

There was no lying to Pa. He'd been a general in the war. An assistant to General Washington. "She was chasing me." I suddenly found the hem of my dress very interesting.

His breath came in spurts. "We'll talk, then."

"Yes, sir," I said.

He went inside. I followed. Martha was still kneeling over Mama, comforting her.

Mama, white-faced, with dark circles under her eyes, reached out her arms to Pa. "Oh, Nathanael, I'm sorry," she said.

Pa knelt next to her. "The doctor is on his way," he told her.

But it was what Martha said that affected us most.

"It's Cornelia's fault," she told him. "She was running away from Mama and she wouldn't stop when Mama said to stop. She made Mama run after her."

Pa went right on talking to Mama, and for a moment I didn't think he paid mind to Martha at all. I thought he scarce heard her.

But, as it turned out, he did. Pa's experience as a general had taught him to take account of everything at once, to listen to what six people were saying at the same time while the guns were booming. And there weren't any guns booming at the time in our kitchen.

CHAPTER THIRTEEN

Pa picked Mama up, wrapping her in blankets that Alice had fetched, and brought her upstairs to their room.

"Go to your rooms and stay there," he ordered me and Martha.

Martha did but I didn't. I set to helping Alice and Polly and Janice clean up. Because it was my fault what had happened. When they wiped the blood up from the floor, I made some tea for Mama, and when the front door knocker sounded, I took off my apron and answered it and walked Dr. Kinney upstairs.

That good man stared at me. I must have been God's own mess. "Are you hurt, Cornelia?" he asked.

"No, sir, my mama is. I was just making her some tea."

He nodded and went into Mama and Pa's bedroom. "You're a good girl," he mumbled. It comforted me, his saying that. If only Pa would think so.

As I went back down the stairs, the others were coming up.

George, who was the oldest at almost eleven, born during a heavy bombardment at Cambridge at the beginning of the war and named after George Washington himself.

And Martha, who had come out of her room where Pa had sent her.

Nat came with them. He was near seven, born after me.

Louisa, the baby, toddled last. She was two.

I had the singular honor of being conceived at Valley Forge. "That camp on the west bank of the Schuylkill," Pa called it, "that had no valley and no forge. Your mother was happy there."

"Of course she was happy," Martha once told me. "Surrounded by all those army officers who danced and flirted with her."

Martha seemed to know a lot about it. Oh, there was no mystery as to the reason she knew a lot about it.

Eulinda told her things. In all honesty, Eulinda told us all a lot of things about the war, about the interesting stories in Mama and Pa's past, for as far back as she knew, anyway. How else would we know about "the dark huts and leaky roofs" the men lived in at Valley Forge? About how the men lived mostly on "fire cakes," a paste of flour and water cooked on hot rocks over an open fire.

How else would I know that when I was born, in our Coventry, Rhode Island, home, Mama was in travail for two days. And that at the time, Pa had wanted another boy but he didn't get one until Nat came along. And that somewhere in between, Mama lost another baby to whooping cough.

But always, always, Martha knew more. Because Martha badgered Eulinda to tell more.

Up ahead in the hall, Pa came out of Mama's room. My brothers and sisters were all chattering on the steps below me.

"Downstairs, all of you," Pa ordered. "The doctor is seeing to your mother. I want no noise. Where is your tutor? Where is Mr. Miller?"

"He's in the kitchen, seeing to some food for us," George said. "He wants to take us on a ride this afternoon. Can we go, Pa?"

"No. I'll speak with him. I want you all here, in case I need you. Now go downstairs." He shooed them and they went.

What did he mean, "in case I need you"? Was Mama failing? Dying? A shock of fear went through me. I cast Pa a look of appeal before I turned to go downstairs, too.

He put a restraining hand on my shoulder, then said, "Go in and see your mother."

Eulinda was in there. She glared at me as I entered. "Bad girl," she snarled, "to bring your mama to such a state."

Mama lay, eyes closed, pale and beautiful, in their large tester bed.

To the side, in a white, lace-trimmed cradle, lay the baby. From somewhere, some servant had hastily procured a pink bow and tacked it on the cradle. Another girl, but so tiny you would not believe she could manage to breathe. Yet she did.

"Mama?" I whispered.

The violet eyes looked up at me. "Cornelia," she said.

I could think of nothing to say. My mouth was dry. I needed some water. And then Pa came back in.

"What do I say?" I asked him.

"Nothing. Just hold her hand for a moment or two. Then go to your room. I'll be along when she falls asleep."

I HAD CHANGED my clothes by the time Pa came knocking at my door. He came in, leaving the door half open, and leaned against the doorjamb, looking at me. I sat in a chair, my bloodstained dress and apron on the floor next to me.

I had changed into a calico he'd given me last Christmas. Did he notice? Did he care? "Is Mama all right?" I asked.

"She's been brought awfully low, but she will recover. With rest."

"And the baby?"

"Seven months. Dr. Kinney says she won't make it through the night."

The calm with which he said this shocked me. I think he too was in shock.

"Is it my fault, then?" I asked.

He shook his head no. "We don't play that game in this house. I've told you that before. In the army, Washington never laid blame when a battle was lost. He gathered his officers and made plans for the next one. But I would like to know why you were running from her. That would be a help right now."

Sarcasm. With Pa, it was on the way to anger. I must be careful. "I didn't go to school this morning," I said quietly, "and Mama was after me for it. And so I was hiding from her."

"Why didn't you go to school?"

There was nothing for it but to tell. "I don't like Mr. Miller."

"You don't like Mr. Miller," he repeated flatly.

"No, sir."

"Why?"

Well, there was no telling *this,* now or ever. What could I say? That one day I'd left my notebook in the classroom and gone back for it and found Mr. Miller, all of twenty-five, sitting behind his desk and Mama standing in front, leaning over it, and then him, of a sudden, standing up, taking her by the shoulders, and kissing her.

"I will have an answer," Pa said. "Can you give me a good reason for this?"

Tears came down and I swallowed them back. "Please, Pa, I can't. Please, you can punish me all you want. I can't."

He scowled. Pa scowling was not a thing you wanted to see.

"Has he done something to offend you? Has he acted unseemly toward you? You know what I mean, Cornelia. We've spoken of this."

"No, sir." I started to cry.

He let me cry for a minute, then took out his handkerchief and reached out his arm to me. I went to him, and he gave me the handkerchief and enfolded me in his arms.

"My pa beat me," he said with no emotion in his voice. "When I came home from sneaking away to go to dances, he'd beat me bad. Quakers don't dance, you see, Cornelia, and I loved to dance. One time I fooled him. I put some wooden shingles inside my pants."

My sobbing subsided somewhat. I looked up at him. "You are a good pa," I said.

He rested his chin on top of my head. "Mayhap I should have let the others go for a ride this afternoon with Mr. Miller," he said. "Only I wanted to take you and George and Martha and Nat on a trip soon. To see the land I purchased on the southern end of Cumberland Island. It's a long trip. We've got to take a sailing ship about a hundred miles on the Saint Marys River, then go by horseback to where my land lies."

"Oh! When can we go, Pa?"

He scowled down at me. "Not for a while now. Not until I'm sure your mother is well."

I nodded respectfully. "Is this where you're going to build the house you call Dungeness?"

"Yes."

"And you've got the plans all drawn up for it?"

"Yes."

"Mr. Miller told us you'll never live there."

"He did, did he?"

"I shouldn't tell tales out of school, Pa, but yes."

He released me, but not without a mild shake. "No, you shouldn't. I don't like tales told out of school. I should be punishing you, not rewarding you by promising you a trip. But yes, I'd like to take you. Only after your mother is well again and we see how fares the baby. Do you think you could stay good until then? And go to school, despite your dislike for Mr. Miller?"

"Yes, sir," I promised.

"All right, now I'm going to see your mother. Go downstairs and make yourself useful."

THE BABY DIED before nightfall. And I blamed myself, though neither Mama nor Pa did. But if I hadn't blamed myself, I could always count on Martha, who reminded me before I went to my room that night.

"Well, I hope you're proud of what you did this day. It's all your fault, you know, that we lost our little sister."

CHAPTER FOURTEEN

WE BURIED the baby the next day, in the small cemetery plot Mama and Pa had on Mulberry Grove.

Mama was not in attendance. She stayed in bed, Eulinda by her side. The rest of us gathered round the small coffin. And all the slaves sang their songs to oblige Pa, but I knew the sad cadence of these spirituals only brought him lower than he needed to be.

When Pa and Mama had lived up north, they'd never had any slaves. They did not believe in slavery. But after the war, Pa had no money. He'd given thirty thousand pounds sterling to merchants to cover debts because they'd supplied his troops with clothing and other necessities. All his wartime investments went bad. His privateers lost fortunes. The iron furnace showed no profit.

That's what Mama had told us.

That's when the Georgia legislature gave him Mulberry Grove.

Pa had once written to his friend Abel Thomas, a Philadelphia Quaker, *On the subject of slavery, nothing can be said in its defense.*

And then, of a sudden, he had Mulberry Grove, which had more than 1,300 acres and included "fine river swamp" for cultivating rice, and a "very elegant house."

South Carolina gave him a plantation called Boone's Barony, 6,600 acres on the Edisto River. And ten thousand guineas to go with it. *The land without means of cultivation will be but a dead interest,* Pa wrote when he petitioned the South Carolina legislature to buy the Negroes that went with Boone's Barony.

Pa came to realize that you could not have plantations without slaves to run them.

He began buying more slaves.

He had to make a trip to Philadelphia, where he wanted to buy fifty-eight more slaves for Mulberry Grove. He refused to pay more than sixty pounds sterling per person.

He now had a slave broker. The man advised him that the prices he wanted to pay were far too low: *Common field negroes sold at St. Augustine for 50 pounds to 70 pounds sterling, and on credit, of course, they sell much higher. The lowest terms that have been offered were 70 pounds per head for a gang of 72, viz. 25 men, 24 women, & 23 children,* the man wrote, advising Pa.

Pa paid a just price, though it was more than he wanted to, and purchased fifty-eight Negroes in Philadelphia and had them conveyed to his estate in Georgia.

By that spring, the slaves had two hundred acres planted

in rice and corn. And it looked, Mama said, as if the plantation would start to pay for itself.

I CRIED ALL through the funeral for the baby. And just before it, I marched myself into Pa's library and made a demand of him.

He was bending over his desk, writing something. He looked up. "What is it?" he asked.

"The baby has to have a name," I told him.

From wherever he was in his mind, he brought himself forward. He straightened up and stood, pen in hand. "A name?" he asked.

"Yes, sir. She can't be buried without a name. What is it to be?"

He gave a heavy sigh. He closed his eyes for a moment. "She only lived a few hours, Cornelia."

"Please, Pa, she has to have a name. Didn't you and Mama give her one?"

They had not. I could see that now.

"Why is it so important to you?" he asked.

"Because she would be alive if not for me. I killed her."

"Don't say that."

"I did, Pa."

"I heard Martha say that to you when you parted before going to bed last night. And I'm going to have a firm word with that young lady about it. I will not have you living with that on your conscience. And I do not want to hear that out of you again. Do you understand?"

"Yes, sir."

He nodded, slowly. "Very well, if it makes you feel better, you may give the baby a name. I have to enter something in the family Bible anyway. What will it be?"

"You want me to pick it?"

"What will it be?"

I thought for a minute. "Virginia," I said. "Do you think that will be acceptable to Mama?"

"You are never to mention it to your mother. Or anyone. Now go out to the cemetery. I'll be right along."

TOWARD THE END of the war, Pa had asked to be put in charge of the whole southern campaign. General Washington, by order of Congress, had given it to him.

Somehow the South got a grip on Pa's soul, because he has the kind of soul you can get a grip on if you have a worthy cause.

After the Georgia legislature gave him Mulberry Grove, he invested his money in seven thousand acres of land on Cumberland Island, off the coast of Georgia. And he drew up plans for a house, not yet built, that he called Dungeness.

More a castle, it appeared from his drawing, four stories high, with thirty rooms and a tower on top. He wanted it made of tabby, which is a mixture of concrete and oyster shells. The walls, Pa said, would be six feet thick. He told us too that the land around it had acres and acres of oak and pine trees that he wanted to make into timber.

In a house that big, I could certainly find a room where nobody could seek me out, I decided, and I could not wait to go with Pa and the others on the trip to see the land.

WHEN THE FUNERAL was over, Pa gave orders that we were to attend school. It was no holiday and it shouldn't be treated like one.

"That means you too, Cornelia," he said. "And I'll tolerate no less."

I went to the classroom faithfully over the next two weeks, but I could not concentrate on my work. I seemed to fall into a morose stupor. A terrible sadness overtook me like the fog that sometimes lays over the edge of the Savannah River, just a hundred yards from our house.

Twice in these two weeks, Martha reminded me that I was responsible for the death of the baby.

It preyed on my mind.

Sometimes I would just stare out the windows of our house at the great marshy wilderness of the rice fields. Sometimes I would watch my brother George tramping through the cornfields with Pa. George and Pa often walked through the cornfields together. No doubt Pa was teaching George things, things he had no call to teach the rest of us.

At table one evening I paused, fork in hand, and stopped chewing.

"Cornelia," Mama said, "what is wrong? What's ailing you?"

"I was just wondering what this place was like when it was a silkworm farm."

Pa fastened his gaze on me. He sensed something was amiss and he knew what it was. He knew I was still blaming myself for the death of the baby.

After supper that very night, he summoned both Martha and me into his library.

We stood there before his desk, much like two soldiers who had fallen asleep on guard duty, both sensing the worst.

"I have a sense of what is going on," he said. "And it is getting tedious. Nothing is more painful than for me to see you two girls fighting. Martha, how many times since the death of the baby have you told your sister that she is to blame for this tragedy?"

"I never said such," Martha lied.

Pa slapped his palm on the desk. "Do *not* make so bold as to lie to me! I heard with my own ears you say these words to her the night the baby died."

From the corner of my eye I saw Martha's face go white.

"How many times since?" Pa asked again.

Martha kept a still tongue in her head.

"Cornelia?" Pa's gaze then was directed at me.

I lowered my eyes and refused to answer. I would not tell tales out of school. And if he punished me, so be it.

Pa saw his predicament. "From the observations I am able to make, I can see that you, Cornelia, are being continually brought low by circumstances your sister will not allow you to escape from. Martha, never in all my born days did I ever suspect you to be so unkind. I have not forgotten, lest you think I have, the terrible day your mother lay on the floor in the kitchen, badly injured, and I came to her aid. Before you said anything to me, you told me that it was all Cornelia's fault. In a time of family crisis your first thought was to lay blame."

Nobody said anything for a moment.

Then Pa spoke again. "You know, Martha," he said quietly, "the first time I saw you, you were over a year old. I rode one hundred and seventy miles, from White Plains, New York, to Coventry, Rhode Island, in two nights and three days. It was July of 'seventy-eight. I had not seen your mother since Valley Forge, winter of 'seventy-seven. George was two and a half and he scarce knew me. I had a day to spend with my family before I had to return to war. You were not a healthy child. You had what they call rickets. Perhaps, I mind now, I was away from my family too much, at war too much, for me to impart my values to you."

"Pa," Martha said.

"We cannot be divided in this family, nevertheless," he went on. "I thought I had striven to teach you that. I will *not* have it. Therefore, I do not beseech you both, I *order* you both to come about and mend your ways. Cornelia, I have told you once and I will tell you only once again, that the death of the baby was not your fault. It was God's will. Do you think you are God? Do you?"

"No, sir."

"Then let your mind entertain the fact that you are not responsible for life-death matters. Martha, my current sentiment toward you is high dissatisfaction. You have displayed all the qualities lately that I abhor. So you are to be punished. Not out of vindictiveness but out of hope that you will realize how unhappy I am with you and that if you pursue this same line of conduct, you will bring more unhappiness upon me. And yourself."

Martha raised her chin in defiance but said nothing.

"I intended to take you and George, Cornelia, and Nat on a trip, soon as your mother is well, to the land I own on the southern end of Cumberland Island, to see the place. Now the rest of us will go, but you will stay home."

I stifled a gasp.

"Not fair," Martha snapped.

Again Pa brought his palm down on his desk. "Don't sass me, or you'll be confined to your room for a week."

He was not our pa now. He was a general in the army, second in command to Washington. I could almost see the American flag on a pole behind his chair.

Martha hushed. I could just imagine what she was feeling inside. I knew how much Pa's approval meant to her, because I knew how much it meant to me. And if he spoke like that to me, I would melt like a candle and drip into nothingness onto the floor.

He dismissed us then, cautioning us both not to bring our "childish pettiness" before Mama. "She is still recovering," he cautioned, "in mind and body, from her loss."

I WAS NEAR nine years old when Anthony Wayne made his spring visit. For some reason I felt electricity in the wind and decided that Anthony Wayne had brought it with him.

Mama had known Brigadier General Anthony Wayne since Valley Forge, where he had helped save the army from starving to death by making expeditions rounding up cattle and bringing them back.

He had a wife, even then, but she never came to Valley Forge like Mrs. Washington or Mama or Mrs. Knox. Her name was Polly Penrose, and she came from an important Philadelphia family. Early in their marriage, Wayne took her on a trip to Nova Scotia, when he had been a surveyor and agent for a land company. There she was miserable. Once home, she vowed never to accompany him anywhere again, and never did.

Wayne, everyone said, loved women. Mama was fond of saying that he collected sweethearts all over the place and oftimes forgot he was wed.

In the army, Pa had put Wayne in charge of the Georgia campaign.

And wherever Mama and Pa lived during the war, Wayne made it his business to call.

Mama, you see, was one of his "sweethearts." She knew it, and Pa knew it and accepted it. And Wayne knew it, and he respected the boundaries of it because he respected Pa.

Wayne's plantation was now downriver from Mulberry Grove. He came often to call. I found myself quickening and becoming more alive when he did. I was fascinated with his large, capable hands, his manner of speech, his teasing of my brothers and sisters.

He had come to sup with us on this one balmy March evening, and Pa was telling him about having two hundred acres of the place producing rice and corn this year.

"Your gardens are delightful," Wayne said. All the time, he was watching me, and I was looking at my plate of food.

"Yes," Pa agreed. "We'll soon have green peas and as fine heads of lettuce as you'll ever see. The mockingbirds sing, evening and morning. In our orchard we expect to have apples, pears, peaches, apricots, figs, and oranges. And strawberries that measure three inches around."

I looked at Wayne. He smiled at me. "You're raising some beautiful children, too, Nathanael," he said, eyeing me as he said this.

I blushed, then I shivered, then tears came to my eyes.

"Cornelia, you're not eating," Mama said.

"I don't feel well. Can I please be excused," I pleaded, looking at Pa.

He, being the general that he would always be, saw the predicament I was in, in my girlish embarrassment, and said, softly and gently, "Of course, darling."

I fled the table and the room.

Wayne, now separated from his wife, practically became a member of the family. So much so that he came to call without notice, when Pa was away on business. Those times, he had long talks with Mama in the front parlor while she did her embroidery. They talked about the old days at Valley Forge. One day when I came in from picking some strawberries in the garden, the ones that measured three inches around, I heard them from down the center hall of Mulberry Grove. As I approached the door of the front parlor, the talking stopped. The door of the room was partly open, and I found that they were kissing. Standing up and kissing. She held the pillowcase that she was embroidering in one hand as he held her in his arms.

I made a noise in my throat that was involuntary, more of a stifled cry.

Wayne turned and Mama pushed him away. Her eyes went big and she said to me, "Cornelia, don't you know you're supposed to knock and not just intrude on people?"

Wayne took my part. "It's her house. She'll throw me out in a minute. All right, Cornelia, I know when I'm not wanted. I was just giving your mother a polite kiss because I can't stay for the noon repast. I've got a plantation to run, too. Someday you two must come and see it."

He was not to be brought low by a near-nine-year-old girl. He reached for his hat on a nearby table, bowed to us both, and strode out of the room, right past me.

As he did so, he patted my head and looked down at me, this handsome man with the strong jaw and hazel eyes, and winked as if we had some secret between us. Then he walked out, leaving me there to deal with Mama. Leaving her there to make explanations to me, if she chose to make any.

CHAPTER FIFTEEN

MAMA NEVER let a word pass her lips to me about that kiss with Anthony Wayne. And so, in turn, I never made mention of it to her.

It was there, though, between us, like a moth fluttering between two flames, igniting our souls, making each of us remember.

But somehow not as bad as what had flared in me the time I'd caught her with my tutor Phineas Miller in the schoolroom.

I'd forgotten my notebook that day and had gone back for it to find the classroom empty but for Mr. Miller and Mama. She was in front of his desk, leaning over it. He was showing her some papers, and then, just as I came to the doorway, of a sudden he stood up, took her by the shoulders, and kissed her.

There was my beautiful mama, the mother of five children, and twenty-five-year-old Phineas Miller, who hadn't the sense to mind his own beeswax, kissing her! I wanted to storm into the room and beat him over the head or something! But I just stood there. Then, because the kiss went on beyond decency, I cleared my throat and said, "Excuse me, I left my notebook."

Well, Mama got all out of shape and stood up straight and scolded me into next week about not knocking proper-like, and intruding on grownups when they were in conference. *Conference!*

I did what I was supposed to do, of course. I apologized. I said, "I'm sorry, ma'am," like I was expected to say. Then, real wicked-like, I said, "I'm sorry, sir," to Mr. Miller. "May I fetch my notebook?"

He brought it over and handed it to me. His eyes were very narrow and hateful, and I met them with my own, which I made just as narrow and hateful, because I'm good at doing that. And because Mama couldn't see the look I gave him. Of course, I knew I wouldn't suffer for it the next day in class, because if he made me suffer, I might tell Pa what had occurred here in this time and place. And then only God knew what would happen to him.

And afterward, Mama, who was so quick to slap, or pick up a switch and spank, did nothing. Because, it went without saying, I might cry to Pa about it, and Pa did not like his children punished that way, and then she would have to tell him why she slapped or spanked. So nothing was ever said or done about the terrible incident between Mama and Mr. Phineas Miller. And as far as Mama and Phineas Miller knew, it was forgotten.

Except by me. I never forgot it. At first it made me disbelieving. This was my *mama* we were talking about here! My own pa had talked with both me and Martha already about boys and men and how some were not to be trusted and what to do if they acted unseemly toward us.

And then, after I stopped being disbelieving, I knew I had to be accepting of Mama's behavior. That hurt more than anything. I don't know what comes next, after being accepting. I haven't come that far along yet, and I don't want to think about what comes next, because I'm afraid of it. I just want to stay frozen, where I am, in the accepting part.

And then, oddly, it was someone else who brought a rumor about Mama's behavior to my attention.

One day, shortly after, on my way to the schoolhouse, I heard someone whispering my name. I stopped on the path and turned.

There was a disreputable young slave woman by the name of Chancy. I knew she worked on Anthony Wayne's plantation, that she went frequently into Savannah on errands when he needed it, and that she was a carrier of secrets, used by both the whites and the Negroes.

"Miz Greene?" She was begging me. "Cornelia?"

I stopped in my tracks. "Yes? I'm late. What is it?"

She stepped out of the shadows of the orange trees. "I gots to tell you somethin'. My mistress, she kill me if'n I don't."

She considered General Wayne's estranged wife her mistress, though she lived on his plantation more than her place in Savannah, going there occasionally to work for General Wayne's wife.

She gestured now that there was an urgency about the matter at hand and that I should step into the grove of orange trees with her. So I crossed the path and did so.

"Well, what is it?" I demanded.

"There's peoples been talkin' 'bout your ma. My mistress say I should tell you 'bout the unfoldin' scandal. The scandal that says Gen'l Wayne an' your mama been havin' a love affair. An' your pa, he ain't home when the gen'l come 'round. An' word is all over Savannah 'bout it. An' your pa should be careful if'n he don't want it talked 'bout some more. My mistress say this."

"Does General Wayne know about this message you're giving me?"

"No. He be madder than a cooped-up bloodhound not able to chase a runaway darky if'n he know. He throw me offa the place an' I like it there better than Savannah. Mistress beat me. Gen'l Wayne, he don't."

I felt anger rush through me. I could have misgivings about my mama, but I'd allow no one else to. "You tell your mistress that whenever General Wayne is here, there are five children and servants about. And a nasty old tutor always lurking somewhere, reading a book. So how could they have a love affair?" I pushed my face toward hers.

She pulled back.

"You tell her, hear me? I don't care if she beats you!"

"I tells," she said. "I tells."

"Now go," I ordered. "And don't you let me hear such words out of your mouth again about my mother!"

She ran.

FOR A WEEK, I worried the matter like a dog worries a bone, but nothing came of it. And then Pa announced that we were to ready ourselves for our trip to Cumberland Island. Mama was well recovered, and she would be in good hands with Eulinda, and now Martha, by her side.

Martha went about pouting but dared not show any deeper resentment. In private she made only one threat to me before we left.

"You'll be sorry," she said.

And somehow I knew I would be.

We dressed accordingly, for it was a one-hundred-and-sixteen-mile trip. The servants saw to it that I brought along my sturdiest clothes and boots. My straw hats had mosquito netting that covered my face. My brothers George and seven-year-old Nat were similarly protected in their clothing, and so, on a morning that began with heavy mists, we boarded a sailing ship at the Savannah docks for the hundred-mile trip on the Saint Marys River to the port of Saint Marys.

The mist soon cleared and the sun shone, and we were no longer ghosting down the river but sailing along smoothly.

It was my job to see to little Nat, and though I seldom speak of him, I believe he was my favorite sibling. And I sometimes think that Pa, for all his fellowship with George, did not realize how smart Nat was.

For one thing, his mind was forever busy, forever figuring things out.

At seven, he knew how to work the loom that Eulinda insisted on using. And one day when it would not work, it was he who figured out what was wrong with it.

He would sneak into George's room to investigate his books, because his own cache of books was already boring him. Sometimes he would trail after George and Pa when they tramped through the fields, a bit behind them to be sure, but not so far behind that he could not hear their conversation.

Mostly they ignored his presence.

The whole business wrung drops of blood from my heart.

Nat opened his own heart and his mind to me, always, because he trusted me. As we walked the deck of the sailing ship, he asked, "Why does Mr. Miller say that Pa will never live at Dungeness?"

"Mr. Miller is jealous of Pa," I told him.

"Because he is sweet on Mama?" he asked.

The question was like a bolt of lightning that ran through me. I could not be less than honest with this sweet boy.

"Yes," I answered, "but we must never tell Pa this. It would hurt him so."

He nodded his head gravely but said nothing.

In his mind he is twenty years old, I told myself. *And I must always protect him.*

On the ship, after we ate our noon meal, Pa showed us his sketches of the house he planned. It was nothing less than beautiful. There would be polished wainscoting, a marbleized banister, four chimneys, sixteen fireplaces, and twenty rooms above the first floor. On the first floor were the two parlors, the conservatory, the library, dining room, and Pa's study.

"Can I pick out my own room?" I asked Pa.

"You all can," he promised.

I chose one in a tower, on the fourth floor.

"Wandering bands of Indians once lived on the island," Pa told us. "Now it is home to deer, pigs, cattle, and wild horses. Pay no mind to the wild horses if you see them. They roam the beach and you cannot approach them. They are very sad-eyed for some reason."

Mayhap, I thought, they are like our family, with hearts full of secrets. Like Pa, whose heart is full of cannon shots and screams of war, and fear that he will lose his wife to Phineas Miller or Anthony Wayne. Or Mama, whose heart is full of the temptation of a hazel-eyed man, or the memory of the final sighs of a baby.

Or little Nat, who is sad-eyed because his pa does not know him for what he truly is. Or myself, who knows too much and cannot tell. And still knows, despite what Pa says, that she is responsible for the death of the baby.

WE STAYED overnight on the sailing ship. Pa and George had one room, and Nat begged to room with me, so Pa said yes. We had bunks, and I let him have the top one. I think the little fellow was lonely.

Around noon the next day, we arrived at the port of Saint Marys, where we had to rent horses for the seven-mile trip to Pa's land. Since Pa insisted we take our time and explore the scenery, it took us about two hours. We went through incredible marshes and lush land brimming with wildlife. I saw colorful birds I had never seen before, hundreds of deer, dark forests of pine and oak, all hung with heavy gray Spanish moss.

We saw what Pa described as "tropical and semitropical plants."

"Sage palms," he described them, "fig trees, rubber plants, and look there. Portuguese laurel." And on and on he went.

Soon we came to Pa's land, which comprised almost the entire southern end of the island. It had large spots filled with virgin oak and pine trees.

Pa dismounted his horse and had us do the same. There was a natural pool of water nearby. He told George to water the horses and tether them to some nearby trees. He showed us just where the house would stand, then allowed us to scout around.

"Don't wander too far," he warned. "Nat, stay with Cornelia."

After a while I sat under some orange trees on some sweet grass where I could keep an eye on Nat, who had gone down to the pool. I lay my head back and closed my eyes, listening to the myriad sounds of birdsong. In a moment or two I felt someone staring at me.

Pa? Nat? I'd just pretend to be asleep. Then I felt a touch, softer than velvet, on my arm. No, a *nuzzle!*

My eyes flew open and I was staring up into the face of a *horse.* One of those horses Pa had said would never let you approach them. One of those sad-eyed creatures. I let it nuzzle my arm a bit. Then, with as little movement as I could, I raised my hand without moving my elbow and patted its nose. It whinnied.

I whispered to it, like I did to my own horse at home. Its eyes were beautiful, like two cups of tea before they were polluted with milk. It made a deep sound in its throat and I listened.

"Where are the rest of you?" I asked softly. "Did only you come to visit? Do you want to be friends? Well, all right, we can do that."

It looked as if it wanted to tell me something. Then, just when we could have had a decent, straightforward conversation, came the sounds of Nat approaching. The horse raised its head, its ears alert, its eyes assuming a glaze of fright.

"Go," I said, "go quickly. And tell the others we'll be back again, and when we do come back, we'll never hurt you. We mean you no harm. And you can always come first, just to me, to make sure. I'll be waiting for you."

The horse whinnied again in farewell, understanding, then turned, soft-footed, and disappeared into the orange trees.

Nat saw it. I know he did. Nat did not miss much. "You were talking to that horse," he said.

"Yes."

"I stayed back because I didn't want to interrupt the conversation."

"You're a good brother."

"Can I stay by the pool a little longer? There are some interesting fish I'd like to study for a while."

I looked around for Pa. There he was, a short distance away, sitting on an overturned log near some clove and fig trees.

"All right, but don't fall in."

"I can swim."

"Don't fall in anyway. I'll be right over there, with Pa."

As I approached Pa, I saw that his back was toward me, that his elbows were on his knees, his head in his hands. He was crying.

I stopped in my tracks.

Pa *crying*?

The man who had served second in command to General Washington in the war? The man whose face represented to all of us courage and strength and the ability to hold us all together?

"Pa?" I asked as I ventured forward. "Pa, are you all right?"

He wiped his face with his large handkerchief. "Of course I'm all right, Cornelia. Isn't a man allowed a few private tears on occasion? Do you think women have a corner on them?"

"No, sir."

He reached out and I went to him. "I was hoping to be able to get you alone for a few minutes on this trip, to speak with you, and yes, it has something to do with the reason I'm shedding a few tears. I hear you were paid a visit by that reprobate slave girl Chancy."

Oh, I thought, and I shivered, dreading what was coming.

But he smiled. "She had the insolence to approach me, too. Told me you threw her off the place. Good for you! But this business about your mother and General Wayne. You don't believe it, do you, Cornelia?"

"No, sir," I said quickly.

"It's being spread by Wayne's wife out of jealousy. Wayne and your mother were friends at Valley Forge, where your mother's high spirits brought happiness wherever she went. General Washington considered her a boon and said she gave the men an excellent outlook. He wanted her around. I always trusted her with the men there, including Wayne, and I trust Anthony Wayne with her today. No matter what that obnoxious Chancy says."

"Yes, sir," I said.

"Today, her spirits are cast down after losing the babe. And it is she who needs her outlook lifted. And Anthony Wayne serves to lift it. I am indebted to him for doing so. And I was crying, yes, because people are putting a degrading meaning on it. And I want to make sure you are not."

"Oh, Pa!"

"People don't know, you see," he said, "what we endured at Valley Forge. The friendships we formed. The uncommon agony we tolerated. It bonded us forever."

He turned to me then. He smiled at me, and once again I saw the strength I had always seen in his face, the strength I had always depended upon.

"So what do you think of this place, then?" he asked, giving the conversation a new turn.

"Oh, Pa, it's lovely. It's the most gorgeous land I've ever seen!"

I hugged him. And he returned the hug. But it was more than any old ordinary hug like he'd ever given me. It said more. He held me longer, with more meaning, with unspoken words that said, "It'll be all right, daughter. I know *you* understand. I know I can always depend upon you to believe me."

CHAPTER SIXTEEN

WHEN WE RETURNED to Mulberry Grove all seemed well. Mama was cheerful and able to be around and about as usual. Anthony Wayne was there, visiting, *lifting her spirits*. The house was in order, and Pa, having inspected the gardens, immediately pronounced them "delightful."

That very afternoon, while Pa and General Wayne were out tramping about, George, Nat, and I sat with Mama by the window that overlooked the Savannah River and told her about our trip and the land where our summer retreat would someday be.

"And we've all picked out our rooms already," Nat told her. "Cornelia's is on the fourth floor. In the tower."

I wished he hadn't said that, because Martha was playing the piano across the room, softly, even as we spoke. She stopped abruptly when she heard that.

"Not fair," she said. "I didn't get a chance because I wasn't there. Maybe I would have wanted that room. I am, after all, the oldest girl!"

And she dashed out of the parlor angrily.

Later, we had a welcoming-home supper and Martha did not come to table.

"Where is she?" Pa asked.

"In a pout," Ma told him, "because she learned that Cornelia already picked out her room from your drawing and she did not get a chance to pick out hers."

Pa sighed. "Have I come home to this, then?"

General Wayne tried to conceal a smile. "She's been put out, of late, because you would not take her on the trip, Nathanael. I would consider it a favor if you would allow me to go and fetch her."

"No," Pa said. "A man of your stature should not be made to beg a spoiled little girl to do what she is supposed to do. George, go and fetch your sister. And tell her if she does not come down immediately, she will find matters most disagreeable. And if she pouts upon coming to table, she will eat in her room for a week."

"Yes, sir." George went, and within five minutes, he had Martha in tow.

Somehow, George could always make sense of matters to us. Martha not only came to table, she apologized for being late and she behaved most admirably.

But later that night I paid for it.

When I was readying myself for bed that beautiful June night, Martha came into my chamber.

"The room on the fourth floor will be mine," she said. "If I went on that trip, I would have chosen it. As the oldest girl, I have that right."

I was fixing the pillows on my bed. "Pa said I could have it. I chose it first."

"We'll see." She stood there like a vision of innocence

itself, in her summer nightgown, which was trimmed with ruffles. "The house isn't even built yet. A lot of things can transpire between now and the time it is built."

"What does that mean?"

"Just that a lot of things could change in the course of time." She eyed me steadily. A warm breeze came in through my open window and stirred the folds of her long nightgown.

Now, of a sudden, she appeared downright ghostly, standing there. I shivered, feeling a premonition of fear. "What are you talking about, Martha?" I demanded again.

"Mr. Miller said Pa will never live at Dungeness. You heard him."

"Mr. Miller is a fool."

"I'm going to tell Pa you said that."

"I don't give a cat's meow. He's jealous of Pa is all."

"What do you care? Pa isn't your pa anyway."

Something dropped—no, *smashed*—inside me. "What? What are you saying now?"

Her smile was no smile at all, but some evil line of glee the devil had sketched across her face.

"I said he isn't your pa. I know it to be true. It's about time you were told."

I moved toward her.

She stood fast. "Do you want to know who is?"

I could not answer. I did not have to.

"You were conceived at Valley Forge. Mama flirted like crazy at Valley Forge."

Here it was again. Valley Forge. Funny, Pa and I had just spoken of it.

"Your pa is Anthony Wayne. Eulinda told me, and she knows because she was there at Valley Forge, and Mama told her."

The floor moved under my feet. Everything was stuck in my throat so I could not swallow. I thought I was going to faint. I felt my face go white.

But . . . but Pa had told me all about Valley Forge. And how Mama had been so lighthearted all the time and had lifted the spirits of all the officers and how he trusted her and even General Washington approved. And how they all bonded because of what they had been through!

"You lie!" I hissed.

She laughed. "Eulinda doesn't. Why do you think Anthony Wayne looks at you the way he does when we're all seated at table? Why do you think he's always telling Pa what beautiful children he's raising? He means *you! His* daughter! And no, to answer your next question, Pa doesn't know. Mama never confided in him. And you'd better never tell Pa, either, or Mama will kill you."

Now she scowled. "And Mama doesn't know I've been told. Or that now I've told you. She needs to keep her secret."

At the door of my room, she turned, smiling like her old self.

"Why do you think you have hazel eyes when the rest of Pa's children don't?"

Somehow, I managed to speak. "Because Mama's aunt Catharine has them."

"Posh. Of course Mama told you that, didn't she? Well, now I'm telling you this. It's time you were enlightened, since you think you have something so special with Pa. So remember it."

I could think of nothing sensible to say.

"And remember, that room in the tower is mine. I want you to tell Pa you have decided to give it to me, to keep peace in the family. He'll love you for that. Or Eulinda may decide, someday, to let it slip out to Pa that you are not his daughter. You know how she is. She talks so much."

Again I felt my face go white. "It would kill Pa."

"It would not kill him. He's been through so much that hasn't. He'd just dismiss her. She wants to go back north, anyway."

"Why would Eulinda do such for you?"

"I told you, she wants to go back north. The other slaves here found out she's being paid and give her a bad time of it. They steal from her. So I give her a few guineas now and then to save up for her trip north, that's why."

"Where do you get them?"

"Wouldn't you love to know?" And with that, she left my room.

CHAPTER SEVENTEEN

I DID NOT sleep all that lovely June night.

It is torture not to sleep, to lie there in bed and hear the whole house settle down and finally go quiet, to then hear the night birds and the occasional barking of the dogs and the terrible silences that mock what lies in your heart.

Then there is the chiming of the clocks, hour after god-awful hour.

And my thoughts.

General Wayne my father! I had always liked Wayne, always admired him. But my father? That would take a whole world of getting used to!

But Pa said he trusted Wayne!

No, it cannot be. Martha is just punishing me. Eulinda is lying.

Mama would never do such a thing. Pa said he trusted Wayne. Eulinda is lying.

It became a chant in my head. Then a prayer.

Why do you think you have hazel eyes?

Because Great-Aunt Catharine has them.

An owl hooted just outside my window. The clock in the downstairs hall chimed three in the morning. Then nothing.

I DID NOT speak at breakfast, except one sentence to Mama.

"You do not look well, Cornelia," she said.

"I did not sleep well, Mama," I answered.

Pa eyed me carefully but said nothing.

After breakfast, as I trailed after him into his study, he turned. "What is it, Cornelia? Is there something bothering you that you wish to tell me?"

"Yes, sir."

"Very well, I am listening."

"Pa, I want to give my tower room to Martha. She wants it. And as the oldest girl, she has the right to first pick."

He scowled. At first he did not understand what I was talking about. Then he collected himself and nodded. "The tower room," he repeated gravely. "You want to give it to Martha."

"Yes, sir."

"The house is a long way from being built yet, Cornelia."

"Yes, sir. But she wants me to tell you, right off."

The scowl deepened. "Are you girls fighting again?"

"Oh, no, Pa. We were just discussing it and she let me know her preference. And I wanted to keep peace, as you like. So I said she could have it and I would let you know."

He did not believe me. My pa was too smart. His eyes bore into me, seeing through to my soul, so I had to lower my gaze.

"What is really going on here, Cornelia?" he asked. "What has Martha done to you? Or threatened you with? Why did you not sleep last night?"

"Oh, no, sir. Nothing is going on. Like I said, I just want to keep peace between us, like I know you want, Pa. Nothing is going on."

"You aren't lying to me, are you? You know I cannot tolerate lies."

"Oh, no, Pa. I would never!"

"All right. I know you don't lie. Very well, then. You may tell Martha the tower room is hers. But I want you to spend the day in the house and take a nap this afternoon. Those are my orders. I don't like the way you look. Am I understood?"

"Yes, sir. Understood."

Still, before I left the room, he gave me a perplexed look, as if he did not believe me, or as if there was something I was not telling him. And it hurt me not to be honest with Pa. And I hated Martha with a vehemence for making me enter into this deceit.

CHAPTER EIGHTEEN

F OR DAYS I stayed to myself. I pleaded feeling wretched. But I found that staying in the house, as Pa had ordered, gave me an excuse to keep away from others. I did not want to associate with anyone.

Mama pronounced that I had nothing serious and allowed me to occupy the window seat where she usually sat and rested. It was the one that overlooked the Savannah River. She liked to sit there and watch my brother George swim. Sometimes, with the help of several Negro boys his own age, he launched rafts and poled them at the river's edge.

Mama would watch nervously. She had a horrible fear of water. She was afraid of drowning, she told me. And I had to admire the way she never imparted that fear to George.

On the eleventh of June, Pa and Mama took a trip to Savannah to see the Pendletons. He had been an aide of Pa's since the siege of Boston in the war. He had spent four years as a prisoner of the British, and then been on Pa's staff in South Carolina. They planned on staying with the Pendletons a day or so, then going on to visit the plantation of Mr. William Gibbons, another friend of Pa's.

Before they left, Martha went on a morning horseback ride with Pa.

It was always a special privilege when one of us was invited on a horseback ride alone with Pa. If we'd been naughty, it meant we were forgiven. If he wanted to "hold forth" on a subject that pertained to one of us specifically, he would use this time to do it. And if he felt he'd been neglecting one of us, this could be a reason for it, too.

I was wild with trying to ponder the reason, and when she came back, Martha's nose was so far in the air that sparrows could make a nest in it.

AROUND THE FIFTEENTH of June, I was sitting at the window seat, where I'd been languishing since Mama and Pa had left, watching my brother George and the Negro boys, who seemed to be having so much sport. I promised Mama I would watch George while she was gone and fetch someone if he got into trouble on the river.

General Anthony Wayne was staying with us, left in charge by Pa.

George was nearing twelve now, his shoulders broadening, growing already into a young man, well able to take care of himself.

I sipped tea, I read. I enjoyed my solitude. And my spirit was still low.

I had not seen Martha for four days now, except at table, for General Wayne insisted we keep the routine of the household going and take meals together, even with little Louisa. She pleasured him, Louisa did. He had great patience with her toddler ways.

Of course, we must have conversation when we dined.

Martha and I made a good attempt at it, although I think General Wayne saw through our falseness.

Otherwise I stayed away from him. Oh, I was polite. I called him "sir" as I was supposed to. I answered his questions; I smiled when the situation called for it. I obeyed his instructions without question. And then I went back to my place at my window seat.

He left me alone and went about his business, which was to see to the running of the plantation for Pa.

I was lying on the window seat on the afternoon of the fifteenth, propped up by pillows, a book in my lap. *Tristram Shandy*. Although I was excused from school because of my poor health, I still had to keep up with my reading.

I had closed my eyes, my book in my lap, for afternoons the sun favored that side of the house. And I felt rather than saw someone standing over me.

"Well, and I thought you were supposed to be reading." The voice came softly.

The last person in the world I wanted to see!

"Open your eyes, Cornelia. You aren't sleeping. What have you done that you're avoiding everyone and pretending to be sick?"

I felt the book being taken off my lap. Oh, God, he was too clever by half for me. I opened my eyes. He was pretending to flip through the book. *"Tristram Shandy,"* he said, disapprovingly. "Isn't this a bit advanced for you?"

"My tutor, Mr. Miller, says I have to read it."

He snapped the book closed and set it aside. "He may be a graduate of Yale, but I always thought he was a pompous idiot. Of course, I can't tell your father that. So . . ." He drew up a nearby chair and sat down. "To get back to the subject at hand. Why are you hiding out in the house on these beautiful June days?"

"I'm not hiding. I've been brought low by some malady."

"And what malady is that?"

"I don't know. I'm just not feeling myself these days."

I did not meet those hazel eyes. I did not, as a matter of fact, look at him at all. I could not bring myself to direct my attention to that tanned face with the strong nose and the set, square jaw. I was fearful of what I would find there.

"Why won't you look at me, Cornelia?" The voice was gentle. It went right into me, probing. "I cannot help noticing that you never glance my way at the table. And regardless of the conversation between you and Martha, even little Louisa could tell you two are at each other's throats."

"Sir, please, I have a headache."

He reached out and felt my forehead. "No fever. What's wrong, Cornelia? Your father asked me, before he left, to cast a special eye to you. He seems to think something is eating at you. Is something eating at you?"

Now I did look at him. There was no anger in his hazel eyes. There was sympathy, understanding, and, yes, love.

"I'm no stranger to heartbreak, Cornelia."

Tears came to my own eyes.

Mama had once told me that it took her years, but she had learned from her friend Mrs. Knox how to keep tears from overflowing and coming down her face. I have tried and tried, but have never been able to master that trick.

Now tears spilled down my cheeks.

General Wayne said nothing. He simply reached for his handkerchief and stood up, bent over me, and wiped away the tears. His touch was tender.

"I don't know what it is," he said, "but if you can't confide in your mother or father, please know that you can come to me. I'll keep your confidences, and I'll help you if I can. I have a daughter, as you know. And a son. And let me tell you, parenting is the most difficult job in the world. Promise me, child, that you won't go on like this. That you will come to me with whatever is eating at your soul. Will you promise?"

"Yes, sir. I promise."

"I'm responsible for your well-being right now. If you honestly are sick, I will summon the doctor. So either get up and rejoin the rest of the world, or I will summon the doctor this very afternoon. The choice is yours. What shall it be?"

I got up off the window seat.

"Good girl." He kissed the top of my head then, and turned and left the room.

I rejoined the world for a day, but the world was not there for me.

I made candy with Nat and little Louisa in the kitchen, because they missed Mama so. I read to Louisa before her afternoon nap. I rode my horse when the sun cooled in the late afternoon.

But the idea of General Wayne possibly being my father was choking me like the Spanish moss on the trees, clouding my vision, getting in the way of my every thought. I minded that I could never go forward with my life, I could never unmuddle my mind and think in a straight line again unless I determined the rightness of the business. And accepted it, whatever it was.

But to accept it, I must know the truth.

And I must know the truth before Mama and Pa returned. So I would not have to look, with a lying face, upon Pa. And with an angry face, for the rest of my life, upon Mama.

And the only one who could untangle things for me was right here, right at my fingertips.

He had said I should come to him, hadn't he? Hadn't he said I should seek him out and confide in him rather than be eaten up? And that he would keep my confidences? And that he was no stranger to heartbreak?

HE WAS ON the back veranda. Supper was long since over. Nat and little Louisa were in bed. George was reading in his room. Martha was upstairs trying on a new dress.

General Wayne was lounging in a chair, his long legs stretched out in front of him. It was dusk, and in the west, the sun had left a few streaks of blood-red stains in the sky.

"General Wayne? Sir? Are you busy?"

"Yes, Cornelia. I'm busy watching the fireflies. I've been fascinated with them since I was a child. Come, watch them with me."

I went over to him and he gestured that I should sit in a chair next to him. I did so. He was sipping a drink. For a moment there was silence between us. Then he said, "Their abdomens glow for a second with a fierce light. They are really beetles, you know. Fancy beetles. Did you know that?"

"No, sir."

"They remind me of certain officers I knew in the army. Plain beetles who put on fancy uniforms and went lighting up the dark and strutting about. Their lights only lasted a second."

We were silent for a moment, then he spoke again. "Did you come to confide in me, Cornelia?"

"Yes, sir."

"Well, confide away, then. I'm listening, child."

I took in a deep breath and let it out again. "General Wayne, I just can't abide it anymore, and I'm going to perish soon if I don't find out the truth."

"It sounds dreadful serious, Cornelia."

"It is, sir. And I hope you won't be angry with me when I speak."

"Have you read my personal papers?"

"No, sir."

"Written to my wife and told her I kissed your mother?"

"No, sir."

"Then, go on, speak. I won't be angry. I promise."

"General, first you must know that I respect you most heartily. But I must ask. Are you my father?"

The night went silent. The beetles whose abdomens lighted up all seemed to wink at us at once. The dusk got one shade darker, but I could still clearly make out his dear face and the expression in it, which was so important to me.

He did not change that expression.

He did not even blink those hazel eyes.

He just gave a small smile, a slight turning up of his lips at the corners.

"Do you want me to be?" he asked.

"I'm not making sport, sir. Please, please tell me."

His face went grave then. "Someone has obviously told you that I am. May I ask who?"

I lowered my eyes and did not answer. But you do not do that with General Wayne. He does not stand for such.

"Look here, now," he said severely, "if you're to trust me enough to confide in me, and you want my confidence in return, let's make it wholehearted, shall we?"

"Yes, sir," I agreed. "It was Martha who told me."

He nodded his head knowingly. "Now," he said, "things start to sort themselves out. So Martha has told you I'm your father. And from whence has she gotten this intelligence?"

"From Eulinda, who was at Valley Forge."

Now he frowned and went silent and turned his attention again to the fireflies. "Eulinda, is it?" he asked. He used an oath then. He took the Lord's name in vain, connecting it with Eulinda's, damning her. Looking back at me, he excused himself for cussing in front of me.

"Eulinda is trouble," he said. "I have long since observed that. Why does your father continue to keep her around?"

"Mama needs her."

"Your mother doesn't really *need* any particular servant, Cornelia. I happen to know she feels sorry for Eulinda."

"Well," I told him, "Eulinda wants to go home. Back north. That's what she told Martha, anyway. The other servants have taken to stealing from her because they found out that Pa pays her. And she's saving up for her trip home."

He ruminated a bit on that, saying nothing. "To get back to the business at hand," he said, "if you believe what Eulinda told Martha, what are you saying about your mother?"

And before I could answer, he threw another question

at me. "Do *you* believe it?"

"I don't know, sir."

"Do you *want* to believe it?"

I looked down at my hands in my lap. "If you will excuse me, sir, that's not fair."

"No, it isn't," he said. "And I'm being overly severe with you. But the charges are so"—he hesitated—"so *sacred,* Cornelia. Rumors always floated around about me and your mother. They still do. You must have heard them. Have you?"

Now I was on the defense, and I had to answer. "Yes, sir."

"Well." He sighed heavily. "Tell you what. I'm going to let you believe what you wish to believe. I'm going to let you develop your love and your trust in all of us as you grow older. But I will be honest with you, and tell you this.

"I will always suffer the misfortune of loving your mother. At the age she is now, thirty-two, she has finally become the finished lady your father expected her to be at twenty-five. He was a dozen years older than her, and sometimes made demands on her that she could not meet.

"Oftimes she did not feel she had the necessary abilities for the role she had to play. We both suffered the disapproval of our mates, Cornelia, and wanted some relief from the oppressive decorum. The war gave us some relief, so we look back fondly at those times. The war permitted us liberties we thought we had rightfully earned.

"But when it was over, we found that nothing had changed. Sometimes we try to relive those times. Like recently, when you saw me and your mother kissing. Many an innocent kiss was exchanged at Valley Forge in the threat of the loss of the war, which would mean the hanging of all of us officers at the hands of the British. Do you understand?"

"Yes, sir."

"That's all our kiss was recently, Cornelia. I venerate your father too much to let it have been anything else. I would never violate his trust. As to your question, *am I your father,* by the gods, you honor me. Come here." He reached out his arms.

I went to him and he took me onto his lap. Pa would never do such. Pa had too much decorum.

"I shall love your mother for all of my life," he said.

I wept in his arms.

"You should be punished for even asking such a question," he told me. "If it is true or not. For hurting all concerned. You deserve to be punished, and so I shall punish you by never answering. You are a spoiled little girl, Cornelia, spoiled as the last apple on the tree."

He held me tight. He did all the things a father should do. He stroked my hair, he kissed my ear, and when he stood me on my feet in front of him again, he put his hands on my shoulders and gave me a little shake and frowned and said, "Don't tell your parents we even had this conversation. And don't let me catch you treating them shabbily because of what Martha told you, or you'll feel my hand, sharp, where you sit down!"

I decided he could likely be my father.

It confused me further. I did not want him to be. I wanted my own pa.

I determined, standing there in front of him, that what I had achieved this night was getting to know him better. I had learned that I respected him, that he was a man of good parts, that if I found out that yes, he was my father, I would be able to accept it.

But not without dying considerably much inside first. Because I wanted to keep my own pa. I loved him precious more. I was not willing to surrender him unless I had proof, and even then it would destroy my soul to give him up.

And certainly I was not going to let Martha allow me to do that without a fight.

No, I needed the truth.

And I would get it. From the one person who had started all this disharmony.

Eulinda.

CHAPTER NINETEEN

I DETERMINED THE next morning, with a sense of purpose that I had not felt in a long time, to approach Eulinda immediately after breakfast.

Of course, I gave no hint of my plan to anyone. I told them I was going directly to see Jenny, our dressmaker, for a fitting of a new dress she was making for me.

Conveniently, Jenny's room was in a private wing downstairs, where Eulinda's quarters were situated. If Martha suspected anything, she gave no sign of it. But she did accost me at the door that led to the steps downstairs.

Smiling. Martha never smiled at me like that unless she was involved in some trickery. "You never asked about Pa's and my ride the morning they left," she said to me.

I would not so much as give her the satisfaction of curiosity in my eyes. I shrugged, trying to show indifference.

"We talked," she told me blissfully. "It was so nice to get Pa away from the noise and chatter of all you younger children. We had a long conversation. We talked about *everything*."

My throat tightened. What did she mean by *everything*?

Did she mean what I thought she meant? Or did she just want me to think so?

"You'd be surprised how understanding Pa can be sometimes," she said. "I hope I have inherited all his good qualities." Then she smiled and walked away.

I NEVER LIKED EULINDA. I suspect it was because she always tried to keep a protective circle around Mama when she was in her presence. She kept a distance between us children and our mother, like a guard, always asking us what we wanted when we came into the room where Mama was.

"She's resting," she would say when she opened the door of Mama's bedroom. Or, "She's reading, and she does not wish to be disturbed. Is it really important that you bother her now?" Half the time, I think Mama was not even aware of this.

Eulinda's English was perfect. I think it was one of the reasons Pa kept her around. Pa was very taken with proper speech, and he would stand for no less from us. If we complained to him about how Eulinda tried to keep us out of Mama's way, he did nothing about it.

"Your mother does need her rest," he would say.

Eulinda would report to him if we sassed her, and Pa would make us apologize to her. Imagine such! Apologizing to a Negro! But we had to do it. Because Pa said that

Eulinda had a history that went all the way back to Cambridge with him and Mama. Furthermore, she had been at Mama's side for those two days when I was born.

So none of us had ever had the mettle to stand up to Eulinda, and she knew it. And when Mama was not about, she bullied us. She scolded, and bossed us around, something I knew neither Mama nor Pa would abide. But none of us wished to make trouble.

Once when my brother George was made to apologize for sassing her, he got back at her. He hid her favorite shawl. She obsessed over that shawl. It was red with threads of gold running through it. Mama said she'd had it since Valley Forge, and she swore it brought her good luck. She'd wrapped Mama in it when Mama was in labor with me. Shortly after, I was born.

It was sacred to her, that shawl. And George crept downstairs and into her quarters, took it, and hid it. Though he full well knew that if Pa found out he'd likely be punished severely. Not beaten, no. Pa never beat any of us.

Well, you would think the British had come back and attacked us again, the way Eulinda took on about missing that shawl. The whole household was in an uproar. Every room had to be searched. George even helped with the search.

I shivered in my laced-up boots for George. *Where has he hidden it? How can he act so becalmed, so genuinely concerned?* Especially when Eulinda pronounced that she knew it had been stolen and cursed the one who had stolen it with the most vicious curse she had.

For she believed in that sort of nonsense. She believed in and practiced black magic. Pa and Mama knew it but did not concern themselves with it as long as she did not do it in front of anyone in the family and kept her doings to herself.

After two days, George spirited the benighted shawl out from wherever he had hidden it, and Eulinda discovered it back in her room again. Soon the incident was forgotten.

George would never tell me where he'd hidden it. But my admiration for him increased. And I knew from that time on that my brother had talents and mental strengths and abilities that others had not discovered in him yet. And that he was afraid of nothing.

I tried to summon forth such attributes as I went down the stairs to Eulinda's apartment.

I knocked on the door. From within I heard her soft voice bidding me enter. I went in.

She was kneeling over her traveling chest, the very one she'd come with from Cambridge so many years ago. She was folding clothing and putting it inside the chest. She barely favored me with a glance.

Since Mama and Pa had been away, she'd not come out of her apartment at all. Her duties in the household did not go beyond seeing to the care and comfort of Mama.

"Why do you bother me?" she asked. She did not concern herself with politeness.

"I need to ask you a question."

"Ask, then, and be gone. I have no duties with you."

I sat down, uninvited, on a chair and got right to the matter. "You told Martha that General Wayne is my father," I said.

She went on folding clothes and putting them into the chest. But she stopped for a moment then and reached for the infamous shawl and put it around her shoulders, as if for protection.

"And so? If I did?"

"Is it true?"

She ceased with her folding. Then she held out one hand. I did not know for a moment why. Then I did.

Money. She wanted money. And if I had any, she would tell me things.

If I did not, she would say naught.

"I have no money," I said.

Her face was stoic, her amber eyes dead. "Then I have nothing to say."

"Do you know what you have done? To me? And possibly to my family? Don't you care?"

"Your family has everything," she said. "I have nothing. You girls have the whole future. I never had a future. What difference does it make who your father is? Your future lies waiting no matter what. I never had that possibility."

She turned from me and went about packing the trunk again.

"My mama and pa have been good to you," I reminded her. "My pa pays you wages. He doesn't treat you like a slave. And I never hurt you, have I?"

"You go now," she ordered. "Leave me be, unless you have guineas to give me for my trip home, like your sister Martha does. You don't know what I have had stolen from me since I've been living here. I might as well be a slave."

"I'm sorry for that," I said, "I honestly am. But why make *me* suffer?"

"Go now," she insisted, "or I will tell your father you sassed me bad, and he will believe me and you will be punished. Go!"

I went. There was no use. She would not talk.

CHAPTER TWENTY

W HEN MAMA and Pa got home, we were so excited that we jumped all over them. Alexis, our cook, had planned a special supper. Pa's favorite: chops and mashed potatoes and mixed vegetables. But Pa did not join in the conversation at table and he scarce ate. Halfway through supper he complained of a headache.

General Wayne, seeing something the rest of us did not, bade us children to lower our voices, to finish our dinners, and to leave the table.

Martha, of course, pouted. Our parents had brought us presents and had promised we could open them in the parlor as soon as the meal was finished.

"Can we open them now?" Martha asked on leaving.

Mama did not answer. Her eyes were fastened on Pa, who said his eyes hurt.

"It's that afternoon sun you insisted on walking in at the Gibbonses' plantation," Mama chided him. "I told you to wear a hat, and you wouldn't. Your chronic eye pain must be flaring up again, darling. Anthony, I think he should go to bed in a darkened room."

General Wayne stood up, taking charge. I ushered

Nat and Louisa out of the dining room. Martha still stood there, waiting for an answer about her present.

George reached out and grabbed her arm. "Come *on,*" he said. "Can't you see Pa is ailing?"

Martha pulled away from him. "Leave me be!"

"Martha!" General Wayne ordered sharply. "Go with your brother. Right now!"

Startled, Martha sassed him. "You can't talk to me like that."

Wayne took two steps toward her. I could not see the look on his face, but in an instant Martha decided to follow us into the front parlor.

General Wayne helped Pa upstairs. Mama followed. I heard his orders for a basin of cold water and soft cloths.

I saw Eulinda appear from downstairs, ghost-like, and follow Mama up.

A few minutes later, I heard General Wayne's voice from behind the closed door of Mama and Pa's chamber, ordering Eulinda out, then her soft footfalls, and the door that led to her suite of rooms downstairs slammed shut.

Phineas Miller read to us that evening in the back parlor. He read from *Henry VIII,* a pompous idiot–like selection, considering the ages of Louisa and Nat. *Yale graduate,* I thought, and wondered what General Wayne would have to say.

I held my younger brother and sister next to me on the Persian carpet as he read. An hour or so went by, but it seemed like three. I was in agony, wondering what was going on upstairs with Pa.

Soon both Louisa and Nat fell asleep, simply by virtue of the droning of Miller's voice, and when Emily, their nurse, peeked her head in the room and saw them sleeping, she picked up Louisa. George did likewise with Nat, and they carried them off to prepare them for bed.

Miller left for his own quarters, which were in the schoolhouse.

I fell asleep, too, curled up on the carpet in the parlor, until General Wayne came down and woke me. "Go to bed, Cornelia. Your father is asleep. Your mother, also."

I sat up. Martha, who was lying next to me, sat up, rubbing her eyes. "I hate you," she said to General Wayne.

"I marvel at the fact that you can find the energy to hate at a time like this," he told her mildly.

I stood up. "Is my pa going to be all right?" I asked.

Wayne's face was grave. "He still had his headache when he went off to sleep. Since my room is down the hall, I told your mother to wake me if there is an emergency during the night. If the headache persists tomorrow, I'll send for Dr. Brickell."

"You'll stay with us, then? And see this through?"

He put his hand on the back of my neck, drew me to him, and kissed my forehead. "Yes, I'll be here. He's my dear friend, and I'll be here for him. Now go to bed. Your mother will need you tomorrow."

Before I left the room, I heard Martha give a disdainful snort, saw General Wayne scowl at her, and say, "Mind yourself, young lady."

She gave another snort before she left the room.

I SCARCE SLEPT that night, worrying about Pa. Oh, I went off to sleep, but soon afterward woke with a start. A thought had seized me like a bear, and I was in its fierce grip and being shaken by it.

Martha told Pa what Eulinda had said. On their ride, the morning Mama and Pa left on their trip. And that is what she'd meant when she'd accosted me right before I went down to question Eulinda.

"You never asked about Pa's and my ride the morning they left."

And, *"We had a long conversation. We talked about everything."*

I sat up in bed. The thought had me shaking.

That is why Pa is sick now, I told myself. *On that ride, Martha told Pa that General Wayne is my father! And Pa brooded on it on their trip. And now it is killing him!*

I pushed aside the mosquito netting, got out of bed, and sat on the edge of it for a moment. Then I heard a noise. Or was it the slamming of my heart in my breast? In the middle of the night, I could not separate reality from fantasy.

So I walked across the hardwood floor in my bare feet and opened the door, not caring whether the noise was real or in my head. What difference did it make, anyway?

Turned out, it was real. As I peered down the hall, there was General Wayne, fully dressed except for his jacket and boots, going into Pa and Mama's room.

An emergency, then.

Fear took over my body, owned it. Was my pa dead? I crept, in my long, thin summer nightgown, down the hallway, to listen outside their door.

There were murmurings. Mama's voice. "But his forehead is swelling."

"Keep the cold cloths on it," from Wayne.

"Oh, Anthony, I'm so frightened."

"Do you want me to sit with you?"

"Oh, I couldn't impose on you like that."

"It isn't an imposition, Caty. You know that. Here, I'll help you keep a vigil till morning. Then we'll send for the doctor. Halt—what was that sound?"

I'd let out a sob. *Oh, stupid me!* In a moment the door of the room opened and he stood there in the darkened hall, a lantern in his hand.

"Who's there? Cornelia? Is that you? Come here."

I went to him, hesitantly.

He stood there, his white shirt open at the neck, his hair tousled. "What are you about, at this time of the morning?"

"I heard a noise. I was worried about my pa."

He nodded, studying my face. "What is bothering you, child?"

I stared at the tin grillwork of the lantern he held. "General Wayne, I fear Martha told my pa what Eulinda told her. And that's what's made him sick. He's dying of a broken heart. Oh, General Wayne, someone must talk to him about it."

"Go to bed, child. Your pa sleeps comfortably. Even if Martha told him, he trusts me. And your mother. Now it's your mother who concerns me at the moment. I must keep a vigil this night with her. Mayhap she'll fall asleep. She needs her sleep. Tomorrow we'll get the doctor. The best thing you can do for all concerned is go to bed. I may need you in the morning."

"Yes, sir."

"Tomorrow, you can tell your pa what a good father he is. And how much you love him."

BUT IN THE MORNING Pa could not talk.

General Wayne had sent, at first light, for Dr. John Brickell and had Emily wake us all early. Before breakfast, he gathered Martha, Nat, Louisa, George, and myself around him in the front parlor.

He told us Pa could not speak for the moment, that the doctor was coming shortly, that as soon as he was finished talking we were to go, one by one, upstairs to see Pa, quietly. We were to smile, pick up his hand and kiss it, tell him we were well and behaving, and that this very morning after breakfast, George was taking us to the Elbridges', a neighboring plantation, so the house would be quiet and he could rest.

We were not to cry or cause him any concern. Did we understand?

We said we did. Then, one by one, the others started upstairs.

General Wayne put his hand on my shoulder and held me back. "You are to stay here, Cornelia," he said.

So GEORGE, capable George, took the others to the Elbridges'.

It was Sunday morning, the eighteenth of June, one of those days God favors us with when He wants to show us how perfect the world can be. All is perfection in His creation, all of nature is in harmony. One dare not think a bad thought on a day like this.

But the moment I entered my pa's bedchamber I knew he was dying. He was lying motionless in the bed, eyes closed and breathing regularly, but his forehead was considerably swelled up.

My first thought was *God, you must like to play cruel jokes.*

Mama was there, of course, seeming smaller than herself in a harp-backed chair. She was wrapped in a blue silk robe. The same color blue formed circles under her eyes.

"Why haven't you gone to the Elbridges' with the others?" This was how she greeted me.

I did not answer, for I did not know why. General Wayne did, and I let him answer for me.

"I want her here," he told Mama. "I need someone to help, and she's the least trouble. Does as she's told. Keeps a still tongue in her head."

I saw Mama exchange a meaningful look with him, but I did not know what significance to put on it.

Neither did I know, straight away, what was expected of me.

"Sit down in that chair," General Wayne ordered briskly. He gestured to a small chair in the corner of the room. "And stay quiet." He did not look at me but went about attending to Pa, smoothing the sheet just under his chin, wiping his forehead with a fresh cool cloth. They were waiting for the doctor.

I obeyed and made myself as small as possible while I looked around.

Mama and Pa's bedchamber always gave me a feeling of awe. There was something so special about it, with the large tester bed usually covered with the embroidery-worked bedspread, the cherry washstand with the blue and white pitcher and basin imported from Holland, and the enormous cherry clothespress in which, I knew, was the blue silk gown in which my mother had been married. In front of the fireplace were the andirons that my pa had made himself at the forge he used to run up in Rhode Island. They had lions' heads.

The whole room was, to me, sacred, nothing less.

Within minutes, Dr. Brickell came. He was white-haired and plump. He had hurried to us and was wiping the sweat from his brow. Immediately, he removed his jacket and rolled up his shirtsleeves, bowed to Mama, nodded to me, shook hands with General Wayne, and went right to Pa's side.

Pa woke, but he still could not speak. I saw panic in his eyes, but the doctor becalmed him.

Dr. Brickell drew some blood from Pa. I could not see the whole business because the doctor's body shielded the procedure, but I did not want to see it. Next he gave Pa some medicine.

I just sat there, quiet and not moving. I think they all forgot about me, and I was just as glad, for surely Mama would have sent me from the room had she noticed me.

Then Dr. Brickell told General Wayne and Mama that he wanted a consultant. "I would like to send for Dr. Donald MacLeod," he suggested. "I wish to confer with him."

So a servant was summoned and an urgent note sent to Dr. MacLeod. General Wayne told me to show Dr. Brickell the way to the kitchen and have Alexis serve him some refreshments, and while I was there to bring up a tray with two coffees, one for him and one for Mama.

I did my task without mishap. Now Pa was lying awake. I appealed with my eyes to General Wayne when I handed him his coffee. And he understood immediately what it was that I wanted.

He nodded yes, set down his cup, took me by the hand, and led me around the bed to Pa's side. "Just one minute, no more," he whispered as he leaned over Pa with me a moment.

One minute! What could I say in one minute? I needed a week! A lifetime! And even then I did not think I could make the words work to tell Pa what I needed to say.

Why, the words had not been *invented* yet that would cover what feelings I had.

Where to start? No matter what I said, I knew that I would spend the rest of my life amending my words, knowing I hadn't said it right, wishing I had another chance.

"Pa," I whispered. "Pa?"

Had he even heard me? I took his hand.

His eyes blinked.

"It's Cornelia, Pa. I want to tell you something. Can you hear me?"

His eyes blinked again.

My heart raced. *He could hear me. And he wanted to let me know.*

Now, Cornelia, say it. What? I asked myself. *The only thing there is to say, idiot, the only thing that matters.*

"I love you, Pa. I just wanted to let you know. And you have always been a good pa. That's what I wanted to say."

General Wayne was coming around from the other side of the bed, where he'd been sitting next to Mama. He was coming to get me.

I clung to Pa's hand because I knew, inside me where

you know such things, that this was the last chance I'd have to hold his hand.

Then General Wayne was standing next to me, his huge, gentle presence hovering over me, his left arm around my shoulder, his right hand over mine, removing it from Pa's.

"That's good, Cornelia," he said. "You did good. Now why don't you come along and let him rest, eh?"

And gently, he kissed the side of my face.

He hadn't shaved yet this morning, and he was always clean-shaven. I felt the fuzz of his unshaven face against mine.

I went with him, away from Pa, who had already closed his eyes. I went back to my chair in the corner.

CHAPTER TWENTY-ONE

GENERAL WAYNE THEN told me to go downstairs and get something to eat because I looked pale.

Alexis gave me some turkey soup and some fresh-made bread and butter.

I love Pa so, I thought. *What will I do if he dies? What will this place be without him?*

But suppose he is not my pa? I minded that while I spooned the soup into my mouth. *It makes no nevermind,* I decided. *For all intents and purposes he is my pa. So why does it concern me, then, what Martha said?*

Because, I told myself, *it just does. Oh, it does not matter as far as loving him. But somehow I must persist in the knowing. Because in the end, for some reason that rattles my very brain and soul, it does matter.*

Alexis asked me if I wanted apple or cherry pie for dessert. I liked both, but I chose apple. Did that mean that I liked cherry less?

If it turned out that General Wayne was my father, did that mean I had to love Pa less? How could I?

It wasn't fair to ask that of me.

I liked General Wayne. I had come to like him more

and more of late. If it turned out that he was my father, did that mean I had to hate him for it?

It wasn't fair to ask that of me, either.

I finished my apple pie and started upstairs. I would have cherry tonight at supper, I decided.

When I got back upstairs, Pa's head was considerably more swollen.

Dr. MacLeod came soon, and after he examined Pa, he and Dr. Brickell went into the hallway and paced up and down for a while, talking. When they came back into the room, Dr. MacLeod said he was going to do something called "blistering" of Pa's temples.

"Do you wish to stay, madam?" he asked Mama.

She said yes, she did.

He then looked toward me. "The little girl?" he asked. "I assume she's his daughter. Do you wish her to stay?"

General Wayne came over to stand beside me. "I'm in charge of her," he said. "She may stay if she wishes. Cornelia?" He looked at me.

I nodded my head yes.

"She's a strong child," he told MacLeod, "and she wishes to be with her father."

MacLeod nodded and went ahead with his work. Blood came with this blistering. General Wayne stood in front of me and said likely Pa did not feel the procedure.

He was, by now, in a stupor, General Wayne told me.

The doctors finished their work, gave General Wayne instructions, and went downstairs. There was, they told him, nothing more they could do.

Wayne nodded and saw them out. Then he came back and summoned a servant, who put Mama to bed in a room across the hall.

"My pa is going to die, isn't he?" I asked when General Wayne came back into the room.

He took off his jacket, which he had put on for appearances when the doctors came. He removed the black stock from around his neck.

"Yes," he said. He sat down in a chair, put his elbows on his knees, and cupped his chin in his hands. "I'm afraid so, Cornelia."

Pa's face and head were still swelling, now almost twice their normal size.

I did not want to give in to tears; General Wayne had told the doctors I was strong. I did not want to be a burden now, to make him sorry he had allowed me to stay. But neither did I understand why I had to be so strong. It was all too much for me, and when tears want to come, something just gives way inside you. You cannot stop tears.

I gulped. I choked.

He reached out his arms and I went to him. He drew me close. "It's all right, Cornelia," he said. "No one is about. You can cry."

I sobbed on his shoulder for a moment and he patted my head and said nothing. There was no need for words. The comfort he gave was sufficient. The man-smells of him were enough—strong soap and whatever he'd used to shave (for he must have washed and shaved and changed his shirt while I was eating). The cleanliness of the new shirt, like Pa's always smelt. I even smelled the polish that one of the manservants had used on his boots.

He wiped the tears from my face and gave me a wan smile.

"What will happen to us?" I asked.

"You will be fine," he assured me.

If he said it, it was sufficient. To ask for more at the moment, I knew, was childish, unfair. I nodded and stopped crying. "Why don't you let me get you something to eat, sir?" I asked.

"That would be nice, Cornelia. And some fresh coffee. Then you should go and take a nap. It's not a suggestion. It's an order."

I got up to leave the room. "I'll be back with some meat and bread and cheese," I said. "And some apple pie."

I NAPPED away that afternoon and woke to find Pa still comatose. Mama insisted that General Wayne nap, too, that she would sit with Pa, so he did, but only with the promise that she would wake him if Pa took a turn for the worse.

That was how we got through the rest of that day, the eighteenth of June, and the night that went with it. The house was very quiet. The servants carried through with the chores. Steps belowstairs were quiet footfalls.

General Wayne asked once to see the Negro overseer, Quentin, to ask if things were proceeding properly on the plantation. The man told him they were and that he was reporting to Mr. Miller.

"Who told you to report to him?" I heard General Wayne ask in a whispered tone out in the hall.

"The missus, sir," came the reply.

General Wayne said nothing except "All right, keep things in order." But I could tell he was displeased about it. That he did not like Phineas Miller was plain, but now I was mindful of more than the ordinary manhood distaste. I was sensible of something passing strange, something almost like jealousy.

What had General Wayne, a hero of the war, to be jealous of Phineas Miller about? There was only one concern. Mama.

Somehow we got through that night. I slept in a kind of a hazy dream in which unpleasant and frightening scenes kept flashing before me.

After midnight, when treacherous things happen, I heard whispered voices arguing. I got out of bed, opened my door but a trifle, and, without going into the hall, listened.

It was General Wayne and Mama. They stood just outside Mama and Pa's chamber.

"You gave him charge of the *plantation?*" General Wayne asked, not believing it.

"I had to, Anthony. You are seeing to Nathanael. It is taking all your time. You can do no more. My God, you can't do it all."

"What does he know of managing a plantation?"

"He's been here for a year, talking and listening constantly to Nathanael."

"You could at least have done me the honor of *telling* me." General Wayne was angry. And I knew, only too well, how the tone of his voice alone could make you know you had sinned.

"I am sorry, Anthony. I meant to tell you. Please forgive me."

Mama was crying. They stood very close to each other. He, so tall, looked down at her. And she, with head bowed, leaned against his chest, begging forgiveness.

But General Wayne, who had told me that he would always suffer the misfortune of loving my mother, did not take her in his arms and comfort her or forgive her. Not then. Not with Pa dying just on the other side of the door.

I loved him then for that. Even if it turned out that he was my pa.

"All right, Caty," he said. "All right. I'm sorry I spoke harshly. Let's go back inside."

PA DIED the next morning, early.

It must have been just after five that General Wayne knocked on the door of my chamber and came in. I was snuggled under my sheet, for I had fallen asleep only as recently as when the clock struck two.

He stood, a ghostly figure, outside the mosquito netting. "Cornelia?"

"Yes, sir." But I knew what he wanted.

"Your father is near to passing, Cornelia. I'm sorry, child. You should come now. For some reason, he has started to talk."

I scrambled out of bed and reached for my robe and slippers, put them on, and followed him down the hall.

Mama sat weeping in a chair. Pa lay in the bed just as he'd been for the last day or so, head swelled, but his eyes were open and focused on some middle distance across the room.

He *was* talking, but it made no sense.

I stood a bit away from the bed, next to Wayne.

Pa's voice was lucid. "A thousand more soldiers, that's all we need!"

"We have them, sir," General Wayne replied.

Silence for a moment or two. Eerie silence. Then Pa spoke again.

"Colonel Rall is dying. Get Washington."

And once more from Wayne. "He's here, sir."

I tried to make a move toward Pa, but Wayne held me firm.

There was silence again while we waited to see what Pa would say next.

But he spoke no more.

Then he took his last breath and died.

His eyes were still open. General Wayne stepped forward and closed them.

Mama's weeping increased. General Wayne nudged me and I went to her, crying myself, and put my arms around her. She hugged me, hung on to me as if she were drowning and I was a piece of wood.

Alexis was there of a sudden with a cup of tea. How had she known? Had Wayne told her to be ready? The tea, I am sure, had something in it by orders of General Wayne, for he nodded approvingly. Mama accepted it gratefully, but her hands were shaking so that I had to take it from her and hold it to her lips so she could sip it.

Wayne was at Pa's desk in the corner, quill pen in hand, writing something. His hand was quivering.

When he finished, he brought the vellum over and showed it to Mama.

It was to Mr. James Jackson, a former colonel in the Georgia Dragoons.

I have often written you but never on so distressing an occasion. My dear friend General Greene is no more. He departed this morning at 6 o'clock a.m. He was great as a soldier, greater as a citizen, immaculate as a friend. His corpse will be at Major Pendleton's this night . . . Pardon this scrawl; my feelings are but too much affected because I have seen a great and good man die.

Mama read it through, grasped Wayne's hand, nodded, and showed it to me. I read it and smiled at him and thanked him.

He sent it right out by servant to Mr. Jackson. On the envelope were the names of the men it must be delivered to. There was a whole list of names.

The other children were sent for. General Wayne gathered them around when they arrived home and told them of Pa's death and comforted them. Mama slept the afternoon away. Whatever had been in that tea had done the trick.

Mama was useless to us that day, so it was General Wayne who greeted the many friends who came to call, the men whose names had been on that envelope, and ushered them upstairs so they could prepare Pa's body and dress it in the uniform he had worn as a major general of the Continental Army.

On Pa's hands General Wayne put the gloves that were a present of the Marquis de Lafayette.

And it was General Wayne, too, who told Emily to pack our clothes for a trip. And to lay out our best clothes, which we were to wear tomorrow, for tomorrow our father's body was to be set in a coffin and put on a boat at the plantation landing, and brought down the river to Savannah.

"For you all and your mother are to go along," he told us.

He told it all plain, but kind. And the children minded him. He told it all as would a general. He would not leave the matter to Phineas Miller.

CHAPTER TWENTY-TWO

PA HAD ALWAYS enjoyed the trip to Savannah. And this day the sun glistened on us and reflected off the water as he would have loved. But to me, the glistening sun had a luminous indifference. It promised nothing.

The men of the honor guard stood around the casket, muskets held firmly in their hands, as if someone would come and steal Pa's body away. The flag rippled obediently in the breeze.

Mama sat near the casket, frail-looking, her gloved hand on it. I stood apart, near the railing of the boat. George and Nat, Louisa, and Martha were at the other end of it, in the care of Mr. Miller.

In a short moment, I heard boots on the deck and there was General Wayne's arm around me. "You're needed, Cornelia, remember? You're supposed to give your mother comfort."

"I don't even have any for myself," I said.

"That's what being a grownup is all about. Giving what you don't have enough of for yourself. Go on now, go to your mother. And don't let me see you away from her again today."

I went to Mama. *Why me?* I thought. *Why not Mar-*

tha? She's the oldest. But I knew why. Martha was about as good at giving comfort as a skunk in daylight. And Wayne knew it, too.

When we finally arrived at the dock in Savannah's harbor, we saw that all the vessels at anchor had lowered their colors to half-mast.

My brothers and sisters and Phineas Miller had come to crowd around me now.

"For Pa," George said of the flags at half-mast.

"Why?" asked Martha, who had never understood Pa's role in the Revolution. Or even tried to.

"Because he was next in command to General Washington," I told her. "If anything had happened to Washington, Pa would have been commander in chief. General Washington wanted it that way."

That gave her a turn, all right. So did the fact that there was no business in town open that day.

There was a whole crowd of people in front of the Pendletons' house, and they parted to let us through. I held Mama's hand, and as we passed, many of the men saluted. The men carrying Pa's casket went ahead of us. Up by the entrance to the house, a military guard of honor stood at attention.

The casket was set down in the parlor to lie in state until five that afternoon.

We, Pa's family, sat down next to the casket while Mama received the visitors. Within half an hour, she fainted and George took her place, shaking hands with people who came to pay their respects.

General Wayne carried Mama to a bedroom upstairs, then came down to help George welcome the people, who seemed to never stop coming.

About five thirty, the funeral procession moved slowly through the streets of Savannah to take Pa to the Old Colonial Cemetery that belonged to Christ Church. A band played, and from somewhere on a bluff, soldiers fired their guns.

There was a simple service in the church. I glanced at Mama and thought she might not have the mettle to make it through. I heard little Louisa whimpering, saw her passed from our nurse, Emily, to George, then I reached out my arms and she was passed to me and I held her in my lap.

She nestled close to me, sucking her thumb. *Poor child,* I thought. *She doesn't even know what is going on.*

Thank heaven, the service was over soon, for it had nothing to do with Pa. Pa was gone, lost to us forever. Where? Into some indifferent density? Or was there really a heaven, a God waiting for him? I shuddered at my blasphemous thoughts and hugged little Louisa's warm body.

They locked Pa's casket in a vault for future burial, and we went back to the Pendleton estate for the night.

GENERAL WAYNE stayed for another week after we got home. He seemed loath to leave Mama, for she was lost in the house, not knowing which way to turn.

We were all lost. The house was an echoing memory of Pa. Phineas Miller attempted to take his place with us, but he failed miserably, so he went about his business of managing the plantation.

In the first day or so, Mama had her hands full with the children.

George did nothing but tramp the fields, like he used to do with Pa. And Mama was terrified with him out there in the noonday sun. Finally, General Wayne had to go out and fetch him in sternly from its noontime rays, for the sake of his mother.

Louisa continually sucked her thumb now, instead of just when she was tired. And because she'd been told Pa was up in heaven, she wanted to stay out on the back veranda where she could "see heaven" and where she would point her little finger up to the sky and say, "Papa."

Nat went missing all the time. General Wayne soon discovered his hiding place. It was under Pa's desk, in Pa's study. He would huddle there, wanting to be left alone.

"Let the children act out their mourning as they will," I heard him advise Mama, "so long as they don't hurt themselves, or anyone else. Don't be so severe with them, Caty. Relax the rules a bit."

Martha, as far as anyone could see, was not acting out her mourning at all. As for myself, I found Pa in every corner of the house. In his jackets that hung in the hallway, his hats on the pegs, his boots that stood ready near the mats by the back door, his gray gelding, the pipes and ledgers on his desk.

These things all held bits of his life in them. They all sat waiting for him to return and pick them up.

And his horse, Tommy, was restless in the stable. What of Tommy? I went to the stable to pat him, talk to him, give him some sugar.

"Don't try to buy him off. He knows." George came to the stall, dressed for riding. "General Wayne says I'm to care for him, ride him. And Mama says if I do well, he's mine."

George had always been a good horseman. With Pa for a father, how could he be anything else?

The groom saddled Tommy, and George mounted him. I watched them argue it out for a few minutes. The horse was accustomed to no one but Pa, and he was persnickety. But George had good hands with the reins, and he leaned over Tommy's neck, spoke into his ear, and the horse settled down. Soon they were as one, galloping off. And I knew that Tommy belonged to George now.

That very afternoon, when we were in the flower garden having an afternoon tea, Martha showed me where her true feelings were. She started in on me.

Phineas Miller was playing a game of chess with Nat. George was languishing in a nearby chair. Louisa was upstairs napping. General Wayne and Mama were sitting near the rosebushes. She was telling him that she wanted to take us children and travel to Newport, Rhode Island, this summer, where she planned to meet with the executors of Pa's estate.

Right in front of everyone, General Wayne took both of Mama's hands in his own and said, "Please, Caty, don't go. My spirits break when you aren't here."

Mama said nothing.

Martha caught my eye, smirked, and, taking my arm, pulled me out of earshot of the others. "Why were you allowed to stay when the rest of us were sent to the Elbridges'?" she demanded.

"To be with Mama," I said. "General Wayne said she needed me."

More smirking. "So you see, then? How what I said means something? And look at him now, begging her not to go. And did you know that he's given Eulinda money so she can leave here immediately if she wants to? Why do you think he did that? So she'll stop talking about it."

"You lie!"

"Ask him, why don't you."

There was nothing for it. Somebody had to slap her. I drew my arm back all the way to Savannah and did so, on the spot.

All blue hell broke loose then. Martha screamed. Mama came running, to find her holding the side of her face, tears streaming down. General Wayne, right behind Mama, saw the whole affair for what it was, observed me standing in front of my sister, dug into the brick walk like a stubborn weed. He glowered at me.

Martha ran to Mama, bawling like a stuck pig.

"What have you done?" General Wayne demanded of me.

I scowled up at him. Then I started to run, right around him, past him, but he grabbed my arm and held me.

"Tell your sister you're sorry."

"It would be a lie."

"Then lie."

"Pa hated lying. And liars."

He grabbed my arm and dragged me along the brick walk into a side door that led into the sunroom. Then he drew back his hand and slapped my face.

"How do you like it?"

It scarce hurt. He did not hit hard. But he was counting on the shock of it paining me. He knew that such treatment would injure not my face but my heart.

"I don't," I said.

He nodded, satisfied, as tears came down my face. And I knew two things right off. That he was sorry that he had done it. And that he would never let me know he was sorry.

"Why did you hit your sister?" he demanded.

"She was making sport of you, of what you said to Mama, about how your spirit would break into pieces if she wasn't here. She thought it was funny."

"It is funny," he said. "I laugh myself to sleep every night over it."

He brushed some hair away from my face and touched my jaw where he'd slapped me. "You see? You wouldn't want me for a father. I'd be too strict."

I just looked down at my shoes. "Can I ask you something, sir?"

"Always."

"Did you give Eulinda money? So she could leave?"

He scowled. "Martha told you that, too, eh?"

I nodded yes.

"Yes, I did. She's trouble, that woman. And your mother agreed. So she'll soon be away from here. Tomorrow, I assume. Yes, she leaves tomorrow."

There was silence between us. We both wanted—no, needed—to say something more, but neither of us had the courage.

"Now behave yourself," he told me severely, "and don't make me have to punish you again." Then he went outside to the others.

CHAPTER TWENTY-THREE

WHEN PA and Mama first came to Mulberry Grove, one of Pa's "extravaganzas," as he used to refer to it, was the carriage he'd had made. Oh, it was not a fancy affair, not gilt and cherrywood, like some people hereabouts have, and you could not rightly call it a brougham, for the driver's seat was not on the outside. But Pa had an extra-large extension built on the back, a place where baggage could be stored, or quilts and other extras, because Mama always had to bring so much along when we traveled. And it had air ducts, because Mama often brought along food and she did not want it to go bad.

"You could fit a person in there," Pa had once teased her.

His words rang in my head the next morning as I watched Priam, the man who drove for us, put Eulinda's possessions into the front of the carriage, then go to secure the harnesses of the two horses it took to pull it.

I never knew Eulinda had so many possessions.

He was taking her to the docks at Savannah, where she was boarding a ship to go north.

The rest of the house was not yet up. It was not yet six o'clock. But I had planned to go on this trip with

Eulinda, to sneak myself into that baggage compartment behind the carriage. For I knew she would not want me with her, knew Priam would not take me without permission, and knew Mama would never allow it.

But it was my last chance to get the information I needed from Eulinda, whom I knew I would never see again. And I calculated that she would be in a good humor, finally going home, and would tell me what I wanted to know. Then, on the dock at Savannah, I would present myself to Priam and he would have to take me home.

I was all ready, even to the buns and cookies I had wrapped in a napkin to take along with me in case I got hungry. Only two things might have hindered me this morning: If Priam had put Eulinda's possessions in that baggage compartment. And if General Wayne had come to see her off.

Neither had occurred, thank heavens. So I tiptoed downstairs, stood waiting as quietly as I could in the deserted hall by the front door, and then, at the last minute, when Priam closed the door of the carriage on Eulinda and stepped inside himself, I ran outside, opened the latch of the baggage compartment, and got inside.

IT WAS A fourteen-mile trip to Savannah, and I got bumped around considerably. But God and the angels must have been with me, because somebody had left an old quilt in the compartment. It smelled of cinnamon and apples, which was not unpleasant in the least, and as best as I could manage, I bundled it up and put it under my head.

Soon enough, bumping and all, I fell asleep and did not wake until I heard someone yelling, "Here, here, fresh oysters, get your fresh oysters, caught just this mornin'!"

I jumped up, hit my head on the top of the compartment, then remembered where I was.

In Savannah! At the docks! I must get out, now! Before Eulinda boards her ship!

Easily enough I opened the door and slipped out, blinking my eyes in the bright sun of midday, adjusting them to the panaroma about me.

First thing I saw was a lady with a dancing monkey and people gathered around her, dropping coins into a bucket. Then the man who had been shouting about his oysters. Another man was selling hot pretzels. All about me there was color to dazzle my vision, in one direction and in the other. On the waterfront huge vessels at anchor, so many vessels, some being unloaded, some being loaded, flags flapping, sailors running about, passengers going aboard, ladies in frocks of all the colors of the rainbow, gentlemen wearing fashions, some of which I had never seen before. Negroes following after them with baggage.

I scanned the area for Eulinda and finally set my eyes upon her. *There.* There at the stall where a man was selling cold lemonade. She stood, sipping some.

I ran to her. "Eulinda!"

Her eyes made the adjustment to my presence. "What are *you* doing here? Did they have me followed? Do they want me back? My passage is paid for. I will not go back. They can't make me."

"No," I said quickly. "Nobody followed you. I hid away in the baggage compartment in back of the carriage. Nobody wants you back."

"You bad girl. You always were a bad girl. Gave your mama two days' travail when you were born. Since then you have been a bad girl. What do you want from me? Why have you come?"

She was wearing her best dress, made of a colorful patchwork of greens and reds and browns. And over it, of course, she wore the sacred shawl.

"I thought, since you were going away for good, Eulinda, since we would never see you again, that you might tell me now. The truth about who is my father."

She sipped her lemonade. Took her sweet time about it, too. The last of it was gone, then she ran her pink tongue across her lips carefully, enjoying my suspense. She narrowed her eyes. "You think I'd tell you that now?"

"Yes. I won't tell anyone you told me."

"How much money will you give me for the telling?"

Money again. "I have no money. Where would I get it? But you have money now," I reminded her. "General Wayne gave it to you. Didn't he?"

Again she ran her tongue over her lips. "Never enough money," she said. "I don't give away secrets for nothing.

Now I must board." She snapped her fingers and a Negro came forward and picked up her belongings and carried them as she walked toward her ship.

"Eulinda!" I ran after her. "Tell me! Please! What difference does it make to you? Don't you understand? If you don't tell me, I'll go all my life without knowing! That isn't fair! *Eulinda!*"

She never stopped walking except once, to turn around and point. "See? Priam is leaving. He doesn't even know you are here. How are you going to get home now? You thought of that, you bad little girl? You're in trouble now, all right. But no, all you think of is who is your father! When you've got everything!"

Then she laughed, waved a derisive hand at me, and, with the Negro following, went aboard her ship.

I stood there, mouth open, watching her as she boarded. I stood there after she was gone. Then I turned to see Pa's "extravaganza" of a carriage drive away from the docks and down the street, and I felt a sense of despair that I had never before known.

What was I supposed to do now? I had it planned that I would tell Priam that I was here. But I'd become so agitated, thinking I had lost Eulinda, that I had forgotten to connect with Priam. And now I was abandoned here on the dangerous and confusing docks of Savannah, a place where ladies never went without a male companion. A place full of sailors on leave, drunks, people with no homes, doxies, and all sorts of undesirable personages.

I must get away from here. But go where for help? The only people I knew in Savannah were the Pendletons, Pa's friends. I would have to walk there alone. And I was not even sure I knew the way.

Well, I decided, *I'd best get away from the docks, anyway.* So I started walking.

I was just onto the street, at the end of the docks, when I was sensible of the fact that I was being followed. Someone was following me on a horse. No, two someones on two horses. I knew they were following me, because horses can go faster than I was walking and they were keeping pace behind me.

My heart was racing. I felt sweat breaking out on my brow. My legs were shaking, but I knew I must keep walking. I would be kidnapped, I decided, wrapped in a filthy blanket and carried away someplace by some horrible thugs. Put on one of those vessels in the harbor and taken to a foreign land and sold into white slavery. I had read about it in books.

Oh God, I prayed, *save me.*

But I would not turn around. I kept walking for at least five minutes, and the two men on horseback kept following.

Then, of a sudden, I stopped. My energies were spent. To what end, all this walking? I could not get away from my pursuers. I put my hands to my face and started to sob. What was the use in trying to get away? I might as well give up and get it over with.

I turned around and looked up at my attackers.

There was only one. A man on a horse, leading another.

The man was none other than General Wayne. He sat his horse under a Mulberry tree, the leaves of which dappled his face.

"Ohhh," I said. "Ohhh, I thought I was being kidnapped."

He said nothing except "Get on your horse."

His face was grim. To say his eyes were not kind would be a generous thing to say. I could not meet those accusing green orbs.

I walked behind him and got on my horse and he gave me the reins. We did not talk at all for the first half-hour of the ride home.

When he did deign to speak to me, we were outside of town and he did not turn to face me at all. "Don't tell your mother why you came here," he told me in an even tone. "Make up some lie."

"So you know, then, why I came?"

Now he did cast an eye in my direction. "Do you think me stupid, Cornelia?"

"No, sir. Not you. Not ever."

"Then do me the honor of not asking such a question. You are as stubborn as a jackass in the mud. And you are going to continue in your stubbornness until you hurt someone. You are bound and determined to do it. You've already hurt your mother. She was frantic this morning, not knowing where you were. Martha told us she saw you sneak off in the back of the carriage."

Good old dependable Martha, I thought. But I did not respond. I took his scolding because I supposed I deserved it.

"I did not mean to hurt Mama," I said.

"Well, when we get home, you're going to have to come with me into the back parlor for a whipping."

I stared at him, horrified.

"I promised your mother I'd give it to you. Because she said she would. She's waiting for you with a riding crop. I said I'd do it." His eyes slid toward me, craftily.

"I said it to spare you. I know what a temper she has, and there was no talking her out of it. So you come with me into the parlor, and we'll pretend that I've given you one, good and proper-like. You'll have to take on something fierce. Can you do that?"

I stared at him as we rode along. And in that moment, he had my heart, this dear man, laying claim to such severity yet going out of his way to protect me so. While at the same time shielding his tenderness toward me so it would not be so obvious.

"I can do it, sir," I said.

"And can you lie to your mother about why you came to Savannah this morning?"

I'd already considered that. "Yes, sir. I'll tell her Eulinda stole something from me. Something I treasure. And I went to get it back. But she wouldn't give it over."

"What did she take?" he asked. "If you lie, you must be able to back it up."

"A cornhusk doll she once made for me. She said it had spiritual properties, then she didn't want to leave it with me. She always said I was a bad girl because when I was born I caused my mama to be in labor for two days."

When I told him that he presented me with a face of sadness and compassion. And having given me that sadness and compassion, he looked like a cat who had just spent one of his lives.

"I hope your father forgives me for teaching you to lie," he said.

"Sir, why did you not think I would come home with Priam?" I asked.

"I had hoped," he said sadly, "to get to you before you even got out of the carriage."

He meant before I got to Eulinda! To keep me from asking what I'd come for!

When we got home, he stood by me when Mama ranted and raved, calling me an "ungrateful little brat" and a "thoughtless, selfish, inconsiderate, infantile being."

I apologized seven ways into next week.

When she asked why I had played such a cruel trick, I delivered my lie flawlessly.

"All this for a cornhusk doll?" she asked incredulously. "Well, you've done yourself in now, Cornelia. Go with General Wayne. You deserve the whipping you're going to get."

I went into my act, pulling back when General Wayne took my arm, but he dragged me out of the room and down the hall into the back parlor, while I screamed and fought him all the time. "No, no, no. Pa never whipped me!"

He slammed the door behind us. We waited a moment. Then he whispered. "Yell and scream."

Then he shouted. "You little devil, come over here! You're only going to make it worse for yourself!"

Well, I yelled, I screamed, "I hate you!" and, "Oh, oh no. Oh, please no! Please stop! I'm sorry! Mama! Help! Make him stop! Oh, Mama, I'm sorry!"

Then General Wayne shouted again. "There, you bad girl, you'll never do that again, now, will you?"

We both stopped and looked at each other. "Cry," Wayne ordered.

So I mimicked some crying and he nodded approvingly. He took off his jacket and stock and ruffled his hair. Then he looked at me.

"The thing is," he said, "you really do deserve it. But I whipped my daughter, Margaretta, once, and she never forgave me. One thing piled on another between us. Things mushroomed and soon we grew apart. Her mother didn't help the situation. Margaretta got married recently, and I wasn't invited to the wedding."

I was honored by this confidence. He never spoke, at least to me, of his personal life.

He looked down at the floor, then at me. And I thought, *Is this why he won't say he isn't my father? Because in some way he wants me to think he is?*

He looked so sad that before he went out of the room, I ran over and hugged him. "Thank you," I said.

"You must be angry at me for a while now," he told me. "And a bit fearful of me. Remember that." Then he left.

CHAPTER TWENTY-FOUR

WITHIN A WEEK, General Wayne went back to his own plantation, counseling us children to behave and to be mindful of the fact that our mother was in mourning. He told George to send for him if there was an emergency, then he got on his horse and left.

Within a week of that, Phineas Miller moved into our house.

We children were confused and in anticipation of the worst. Was this how Mama was to go about her mourning?

Phineas Miller in the house?

We understood now how the colonists felt when Paul Revere sounded his alarm that the British were coming. We crowded around George in whispered conspiracy. "You've got to go and tell General Wayne," Nat said. "It's an emergency."

George shook his head no. "Mama wants it," he told us. "And the general said we have to do what Mama wants and keep her happy."

"I hate him," I said.

"Who?" Martha snickered. "Wayne?"

"Hush, Martha," George ordered. He was a man already. And he knew how to order. "We just have to put up with Miller, is all. Don't pay mind to him when he's about. Just be respectful. Otherwise, ignore him."

"But he's our tutor," I said. "How are we supposed to live with our tutor?"

"I doubt he'll be doing much tutoring from here on in," George said. "He's too busy managing the plantation. Mama's taking us all to Newport soon, anyway."

So we settled down and abided by George's advice. But I still could not forgive Mama for allowing Miller to move into the house.

He brought in all his possessions. He moved his books and papers into Pa's study; that's what hurt me the most. He took all Pa's personal items off the desk and had a servant box them away, and soon *his* pipes and quill pens and papers and notebooks and other properties were there.

One day, when I could abide it no more, I sneaked into the study and spilled it all off the desk with one swoop of my arm.

Everything went onto the floor. I sobbed, doing it, and, sure enough, Phineas Miller caught me in the act.

"What are you doing, you terrible child? You always were a terrible child! I knew you never liked me. Caty! Caty?"

Mama came running, saw the mess on the floor, observed me standing there crying my soul out, and picked up the first suitable object she saw, a yardstick, one of Miller's. And there, right in front of Miller, she bent me over the desk and whipped me with the yardstick while I screamed out for Pa. A real whipping, not like the one Wayne had faked.

By that time, my screams for mercy had brought George to the doorway of the study.

"Mama!" he screamed. "Stop!"

She stopped, grabbed me by shoulders, turned me to her, then slapped my face.

"Mama!" George yelled again. "She's been punished enough!"

She whirled me around then, to face Miller, and made me say I was sorry.

I did so, barely able to get the words out for my sobbing. Then, under her and Miller's watchful eyes, I was made to put every item back on Pa's desk, exactly where Miller wanted them, before I was permitted to leave the room.

George waited for me. And comforted me when I was allowed to go.

Two things became as clear as birdsong to me from that moment on.

One, Phineas Miller had some kind of hold over Mama. And two, Mama was getting more and more severe by the day with her children.

How deep the hold was that Miller had on Mama I did not know. And I had no one to discuss it with. Not Martha, certainly. I would never even approach such a subject with Martha. As for George, he already had the sensibilities of a man, which included loyalty toward Mama. And such a subject as the possibility of a romantic liaison between his mother and Miller would be off-limits for discussion.

So it was left for me to chew it to the bone myself.

Was Miller having a romance with Mama? Did I have to worry about that now? I knew that his feelings were not only alive but growing steadily every day for her. But what about her feelings for him? And now here they were in the house together.

And this man did not have the honor General Wayne had.

As for her severity with us, was she just trying to make up for the fact that Pa was no longer here? And that Pa could becalm us with just a look? Or a word? And she could not?

I did not mind for myself. I could take her critical looks, her sudden outbursts, even her slaps. But I hurt for the others.

For some reason, she decided she must, of a sudden, put a stop to Louisa's thumb-sucking. And she and Miller devised all sorts of terrible-smelling concoctions to put on the child's thumb to discourage her from the habit, especially before bedtime.

George and I took turns sneaking into Louisa's room

at night and wiping the noxious stuff off her thumb. We never got caught, and Louisa kept right on sucking until they gave up their efforts.

Poor little Nat took the worst of it, though, in an event I thought bordered on cruel. Nat loved sweet things. We had a silver sugar bowl in the middle of the table, and one evening when we had fresh strawberries for dessert, those three-inch-round strawberries Pa boasted of so, Nat kept begging for more and more sugar to put on them.

Mama slammed down her coffee cup in anger, reached across the table for the sugar bowl, moved away Nat's dish of strawberries, put the bowl of sugar in front of him, and said, "Here is your sugar. Eat it all."

Everyone fell silent. Nat's eyes went large and round.

"You heard me," Mama said. "Eat the sugar. Every grain of it. I will sit here until you do. Start now."

"Mama," George said.

"Don't you say a word," she flung at George. "Leave the table. All the rest of you!"

We left, reluctantly. All except Mr. Miller, who stayed with Mama, to give her moral support. As we left, poor little Nat was starting to spoon the sugar into his mouth.

George told me later that he'd been informed by Emily that yes, Nat had ingested all the sugar, spoonful by spoonful, while Mama and Mr. Miller watched. Alexis, the cook, had observed from the kitchen and told her that Nat had choked and nearly thrown up several times, but Mama made him go on.

He had begged for water several times. But Mama refused.

Mr. Miller never interfered.

Later that night, Emily came to George and woke him and told him that Nat had stomach pains. George went to Nat, to help Emily care for him, to comfort him.

After that incident, I asked George if he would get permission from Mama for us to ride over and visit General Wayne.

"You're going to tell him about Mama?" he asked.

"I just need to see him something fierce," I told my brother. "Please."

Mama said yes, we could go, without Miller for an escort, only because for a year now Pa had been teaching George to use a musket. He was, as was expected of a boy of his age in the South, an excellent marksman. So George and I set off early of a morning. In his saddlebag he had two loaves of fresh-baked gingerbread, General Wayne's favorite since his army days, and a bottle of wine, all sent by Mama. In my saddlebag I had bread and cheese for our trip and two stone jars of water for us.

The trip took an hour and a half.

We found Wayne out in his cornfields, overseeing his Negroes.

He turned and waved when he saw us, signaled that we should wait, then came galloping along the path that ran by the fence, and my heart beat like a rabbit's in my chest. I felt a sense of hope, as if everything would be put back in place in my world again, that all I had to do was see this man and the cruel joke that had lately been played on me would all be apologized for and things made right again.

After all, wasn't this the man who had gone out from Valley Forge and brought back droves of cattle to the starving men?

He rode up to us, grinning. "Ho, kids! Everything all right at home?"

We said it was. In the stable yard, we dismounted our horses and went with him into the house, through the kitchen, where we were greeted by good smells of things simmering.

We gave him the gingerbread and wine.

"Let's have some fresh coffee with the gingerbread," he told Lila, the fat Negro cook. "And some fruit." Then he led us into a parlor with large windows that looked out onto a lawn where peacocks were roaming about and there was a pool with green plants growing out of it.

The whole place had about it a casual and sort of unkempt look. Not neglected, but lived-in. *Even here in the parlor,* I thought, looking around, *Mama would take a fit.* At the pillows on the floor, at the white cat on the settle, three of his favorite hounds who'd sat themselves by the hearth. I immediately felt at home here.

Over the fireplace was his favorite musket. Others were set about all over the room.

"Are they from the war?" George asked reverently. At home Pa had never displayed guns openly.

"Yes," Wayne smiled. "Go. You can look at them."

George did. He wandered about, entranced.

And while he did, Wayne looked at me. "What is it, Cornelia? Is there trouble?"

Of course he knew there was. "Miller has moved into the house," I told him. "And since then Mama has gotten so severe with us, I don't know what to do."

He betrayed no emotion at the news of Miller moving into the house. He did not seem threatened. I told him of the incidents in which Mama had lost her temper with us, including how she'd made Nat eat all that sugar and how she'd whipped me.

"What did you do?" he asked.

And when I told him his eyes twinkled and he had a difficult time suppressing a smile. But the only advice he could give was that we must learn to abide this, that he would make it his business to soon come and visit, that he would speak to Mama. He promised me that he had an influence on her, that Miller "did not have the chance of a drunken flea with her, though he might think he had."

Lila brought in coffee and fruit and the gingerbread then, and we enjoyed our repast, after which he took us on a walk outside, showing us around. Later we had an early supper and he told us stories of Pa during the war.

Before he saw us off, General Wayne took George's musket and checked it over, pronounced it clean and in good condition, then had George do some target practice. He approved of my brother's shooting skills, handed the gun back, and shook hands with George.

"Thank you for looking after your sister," he said. "I'd be beholden to you if you would continue to do so."

"Yes, sir." George mounted his horse.

Wayne hugged me close and kissed me.

"I'll be by soon," he promised.

He gave George a sealed note for our mother.

As we rode off, I turned once to look back. He saw me and waved his hat, his old tricorn hat that he still wore, from the Revolution.

CHAPTER TWENTY-FIVE

G ENERAL WAYNE did visit again, did talk with
Mama as promised, and for the next few weeks,
before we left for Newport, she conducted herself lovingly with us.

She must have made promises to him, I concluded.
And I knew how that was. When you made promises to
General Wayne, you felt obliged to keep them. He took
hold of your heart, or whatever part of you it is that keeps
promises.

When we left for Newport in the middle of August, it
was General Wayne who drove us to Savannah and saw us
off at the dock. It was he and he alone who kissed us all
goodbye, shook hands with George, and requested that
George take his brother and sisters aside while he himself
stood tall over Mama and spoke low words to her and
held her close.

What words they were I could not imagine, but Mama
was taken by them, for it seemed she knew no other life
in those moments but the hazel eyes and handsome face
of the general, the world he created around her, the promises he gave and required in return.

Then, as our schooner pulled out of the harbor, he stood on the dock, looking like the last man left on earth.

FROM NEWPORT, we went to New York and then on to Philadelphia. Mama had friends all over the place. To my surprise, and without a word of explanation, she left my brothers and sisters with friends in Philadelphia and took me on with her, by stage, to Mount Vernon, to visit the Washingtons.

All the way there she schooled me in how to act.

I was to be the perfect little lady. She drilled behavior in me during the whole trip. She instructed me how to meet every probable occasion that arose while there, from my first presentation, when I must tender him my most profound courtesy even while standing at ease and answering all his possible questions, to keeping religiously in the background.

Needless to say, by the time we arrived at Mount Vernon, I was in a state of anxiety so great that I was tongue-tied and unable to function at all.

Mrs. Washington, a darling of a woman, graciously welcomed us, then ushered us into a ladies' parlor, complete with a fluffy white cat, blue and white vases from Holland, and a dainty pianoforte. I hoped against hope that Mama would not ask me to play.

She did not. And soon the door opened and the general himself walked in and kissed Mama's hand, then threw all caution to the winds and hugged her as a father would have done. For old times' sake, I supposed. For all those memories of Valley Forge.

He offered his condolences for the loss of Pa. He called him a great and good man, as General Wayne had done. Then he looked at me.

"And who is this young lady?" he asked. "One of the many your husband used to beg permission to visit when I needed him so?"

"Yes, sir," Mama said, smiling. "This is Cornelia." And with her eyes and head, she gestured that I should go into my act.

Only I had forgotten what my act consisted of. I just stared at him. No one had told me he was so handsome and had such flashing blue eyes!

Why, he had more of a presence than General Wayne!

I started forward as if walking on eggs. Right about at this point I was supposed to say something, wasn't I? But what? My mind was swirling. I was supposed to curtsy, too. Instead, feeling like a frog on a wavering lily pad, I fell to my knees in front of him and cried.

Mother stepped forward, starting to apologize, but Washington put out a detaining arm.

"Here, here, child." He took out a handkerchief and leaned down to wipe my tears. He spoke in low, soothing tones as he raised me to my feet. He held my hand as he led me to a chair next to his own, kissed my forehead, and sat me down.

"Cornelia, I'm ashamed of you!" Mama scolded. "What would your father say?"

"No scolding, no shame," Washington told her. "Her father has much to be proud of in this daughter. We lost our own daughter, Patsy, you know, some fourteen years ago. Just to have a daughter is God's blessing."

Mama fell silent.

"Now the child is frightened, that is clear," Washington said. "What have you told her of me, Caty? That I put young girls before a firing squad at sunup?"

In the dining room, Washington sat, of course, at the head of the table, and insisted I sit to his right. He saw to it that my plate received everything. He made small jokes and I smiled, forgetting all my troubles. He asked about my brothers and sisters. About General Wayne, of whom he was so fond.

We had the most pleasant of visits. We stayed the night. When I was safely ensconced in my own bed, who but Mrs. Washington knocked softly and came in.

"Child, are you all right?"

"Oh, yes, ma'am, thank you for asking."

She did not leave then, but sat down on the side of my bed. She was a small, stout woman, with such a pleasant face, you had to love her.

"The general, my husband, has headed up many battles, planned many attacks, worked with many men of all stripes. He told me, in confidence, that he thinks that you and your mother do not see eye to eye on many matters. He asked me to tell you that he never got on with his mother, either. But that attempts can still be made to surmount the difficulties, that you must always remember she is your mother. That love is not necessary for this battle called life, but respect is necessary for every invasion."

I smiled. She did, too. And she kissed my forehead. "He thinks you are a wonderful child. Now have a good night's sleep, dear."

I wished, as she left the room, that she was my mother. And then I fell asleep, obeying her and having a good night.

CHAPTER TWENTY-SIX

TWO TERRIBLE THINGS happened during the following year.

My brother George was sent away. And Mama carried on a love affair with Jeremiah Wadsworth, a coexecutor of Pa's estate, the man she'd gone to see in Newport.

It seemed that George's education was on everyone's mind, from Mama's to General Washington's, from General Henry Knox's to Mr. Rutledge's, and all the way across the ocean to that of the Marquis de Lafayette, who served under Pa and was a friend of Washington's.

Washington himself wrote to Mama, offering to bear the expense of George's schooling, telling her, "Entrust my namesake to my care and I will give him as good an education as this country can afford."

Mama was embarrassed, but before she could reply to the letter another one came from the Marquis, saying he had promised Pa that he would have George educated in France, at his own expense.

Mama knew nothing of this promise. Now she was not only embarrassed, but confused. And she would not reply to the letter from the Marquis.

So the Marquis wrote to Henry Knox, asking him to persuade Mama to accept his offer. And Henry Knox did so. Mama respected his judgment, though she dreaded sending George across the sea, convinced she would never see him again.

But soon George's things were being packed up for a trip to New York, where he would stay with the Knoxes until he would sail for France.

He was to be accompanied on the ship by Joel Barlow, a diplomat going to France. Mr. Knox had made all the arrangements.

Again General Wayne saw us off at the dock in Savannah on our way to New York. "Give my best to the Marquis," he told George. "Remind him how we celebrated the French alliance on the sixth of May at Valley Forge."

In New York, Henry Knox gave George fifty dollars.

We left for home before George embarked on his trip. And when we left, my brother put his arms around me. "I will miss you, Cornelia."

I buried my face in the front of his new frock coat. "Oh, I don't want you to go. What will I do without you?"

"You will do just fine. You are growing up. You are strong of spirit. And brave. And you must write to me. Tell me everything."

I promised I would. And he returned the promise. And so it was that I had to learn to live without my brother George.

Yes, I was growing up. I was strong of spirit. And

brave. But that did not mean I could bear having another piece of my heart cut out, did it?

WE WENT AGAIN to Rhode Island that summer of '87. Mama took us to stay with Pa's relatives, who were always kind to us and fussed over us, to Mama's dismay.

After spending just one night there, Mama pronounced that she was leaving us, going to be a guest at the home of Jeremiah Wadsworth in Hartford, Connecticut, for a few weeks.

Pa's sister, Aunt Peggy, in whose house we were staying, looked at Mama with disapproval in her eyes. "I'll wager his wife just loves having you about," she said. "Especially with you still being so beautiful, Caty, and she being nine years older than him."

Mama had told us we must be nothing less than respectful to Aunt Peggy. She had also told us that Aunt Peggy had always disapproved of her.

I watched while Mama faced her sister-in-law. "Mr. Wadsworth is a congressional candidate," she said. "If he is elected, he will present my claim to the congressional body who will soon meet in New York City. Nathanael left huge debts, and I must appeal to the government to be paid back for the money he put forth to equip his southern army during the war."

Aunt Peggy just smiled, very deliberately. "And have

you not heard, then, about the scandal connected with the Wadsworth name?"

"What scandal?" Mama asked.

"The Elizabeth Whitman case," Aunt Peggy said. "She was socially prominent, this Elizabeth Whitman. From Connecticut. And she was found dead in a hotel room, with her dead baby, a pair of forceps, and a probe lying near her bed."

"And what has that to do with Wadsworth?" Mama asked.

"His was one name connected with being her lover," Aunt Peggy answered. "One named as being the father of the dead baby."

Mama gasped, then there was silence for a minute.

"I'm just forewarning you, Caty, is all," Aunt Peggy said. "I think, from the way you run when this man beckons, that he has some sort of control over you."

"No man has control over me," Mama told her.

"I'm glad to hear that," Aunt Peggy said.

"He just wants me to meet him so we can talk about my business affairs."

But Mama's voice was a trifle shaky now. She was not as sure of herself as she was before Aunt Peggy had told her that little story.

CHAPTER TWENTY-SEVEN

"CORNELIA, CORNELIA, please don't let Mama leave me. I don't want to stay here. I want to go home with the rest of you."

We were in Hartford again, visiting with the Wadsworths. It was late fall and, of course, in New England that meant the leaves were gone from the trees. Snow had already fallen.

As if visiting with the Wadsworths was not enough, Phineas Miller had made this trip with us, and the only redeeming thing about it was that he had the decency to stay at a rooming house while we stayed with the Wadsworths in their large, fashionable home.

It was just after breakfast, and Mama and Wadsworth were in one of the parlors. His wife was upstairs, still sleeping.

The Wadsworths' youngest daughter, Harriet, the only one left at home, lingered at the breakfast table. She was all of sixteen. I knew she did not like Mama, that she was embarrassed by her father's infatuation with her. But she was decent enough to the rest of us.

Now Nat came running in from the parlor, where he'd

been the subject of the conversation between Mama and Mr. Wadsworth.

"I don't want to stay here!" He flung himself into my lap.

In this moment, my very intelligent little brother had relapsed into a three-year-old.

"Who says you're staying?" I asked.

"Mama. She says I must stay. Go to school here. Under the guidance of Mr. Wadsworth. Away from rivers and iron forges and cutting machines and the like, so I can grow up whole."

I knew that "rivers and iron forges and cutting machines" meant Rhode Island and Aunt Peggy and Uncle Jacob's house.

I did my best to comfort Nat, but he would not be comforted.

"Well," Harriet said to me, "I heard your mama tell my mama that she's going to put you and Martha into a school in Bethlehem, Pennsylvania, run by the nuns. I'm sure this place is better. I'll look after him."

"I'm not going *there*," I threatened.

"Nothing wrong with it," Martha put in. "Don't you want a good education?"

I made a face at her. And when Mama came into the kitchen, I pleaded Nat's case, but she would have none of it. And so it came to pass that we left Nat in Hartford, Connecticut, and our family was severed even more. And Mama then took me and Martha—

and little Louisa—in the stage to Bethlehem, Pennsylvania.

But before we left, Mama and Mr. Wadsworth had a
fierce argument that twisted my innards, nothing less.

Was I the only one to witness it? I know Martha didn't,
or she would have flaunted it before me. As for Harriet,
well, she was just too proud to have admitted hearing it,
is all. She said nothing.

It was an unseasonably warm fall, and Mama and Mr.
Wadsworth were out in the barn. I don't know where
Martha was—upstairs in her assigned bedroom, I calcu-
late. Louisa was out walking with Nat and the Wadsworths' dog, Buster. I was on the swing on the walnut tree
just outside the barn.

"You are too attached to him," I heard Wadsworth
saying loudly. "I don't like it."

"What right have you to like or dislike it?" Mama
flung back at him. "And how do you know I am too attached?"

"For God's sake, Caty, he lives in your house! How does
that look? And he had to accompany you on this trip!"

"He cares for me and the children."

"Does he have to live in the house to do it?"

There was no return from Mama. Just silence.

Then Wadsworth spoke again. "I have a letter, you
know," he said sadly. "I am in possession of a letter from
your late husband. In it he writes of his concern over your
attachment to this man, *while he was still alive!*"

"You lie," Mama said.

"Do I, Caty? I can show you the letter. In Nathanael's own writing. Do you want to see it?"

"No," Mama said. "I do not wish to see it."

At this, I stopped swinging. My heart was thumping inside me. My lips were dry. *So Pa had suspected Mama and Phineas Miller of carrying on right under his nose.*

And now Mama is carrying on with Mr. Wadsworth!

Does this mean that yes, back at Valley Forge, she had also carried on with General Wayne?

I felt nauseous. The swinging had done it, I decided. Yes, the swinging.

I jumped down and ran into the house.

AT THE ACADEMY for Girls in Bethlehem, Mama and Martha and Phineas Miller were thrilled with the place.

I was not. First off, I saw the wrought-iron bars on the windows. Then the single, sparse beds in single, sparse rooms that boasted crosses on the walls and one small braided rug to kneel on to say prayers.

Where did one put books? Or favorite childhood dolls one might bring along for company? Where was the room for one's trunks? Where did one hang dresses, line up one's shoes?

My questions were answered by a nun with a face so plain that in itself it held the answers.

No books were allowed except those dispensed in the classrooms. You could not read what you wanted. No dolls. They were graven images. One's trunk went home with one's family. No need for extra dresses or shoes. One wore uniforms and the shoes required. As for food, there was no sugar in the diet, no salt, meat only twice a week, no butter, and definitely no tea.

Tea, I thought. It rang some bell inside my head.

When the nun left us, I told Mama this: "I'm not going here. If you make me go here, I'll do terrible things. I'll disgrace you, and you'll have to come and take me home, anyway."

Mama knew I meant it. So we left Martha, and she took me and Louisa on home.

Mama's worst fear was to be disgraced by us children.

To say she was unhappy with me did not cover the situation. No words could do the situation justice. But she took me home just the same.

I would rather suffer her anger and dissatisfaction, which I usually suffered anyway, than live in a place that took away my independence.

After all, Pa had fought for my independence, hadn't he?

WE WOULD have been home for Christmas, which I had always loved at Mulberry Grove, but no, Mama had to make a stop at Charleston, where we stayed with the Rutledges. All but Phineas Miller. He went on home.

This time it was all business, for Mr. Rutledge was

coexecutor of Mama's estate, too, and though there were parties given in her name to which many of the ladies from the "noble families" came and I was forced to attend, Mama and Mr. Rutledge spent many hours in his office, conferring.

Mr. Rutledge, not yet forty, had signed the Declaration of Independence. His name was right below that now famous "J" of John Hancock.

He was a dear man, white-haired, and with no pretense about him at all.

He had been a prisoner of the British, in east Florida, at the fall of Charleston, and as a result of it, he limped and used a cane. But he would not talk about his imprisonment or his injury. He just smiled and went on being pleasant the whole time of our visit. He made it plain that he had always reverenced Pa.

But because of this visit, which went on longer than Mama anticipated, Mama and I and little Louisa found ourselves on a coastal schooner on Christmas Day of 1788. Of course there were festivities on the schooner, but outside, it was snowing and the water was rough. And all I could wonder was *What happened to our family?*

Where was George this Christmas Day? And what was little Nat doing? Was he crying? And, even though I had no great love for Martha, were the nuns at the academy allowing her to have sugar and tea this day?

And, oh, I missed Pa so! At home, at Mulberry Grove, when he was with us, we'd have such a wonderful celebration. George and Martha and I would have the house decorated, and we'd help Alexis bake cookies. There would be special aromas coming out of the kitchen. The table in the dining room would be groaning with all the food. There would be a tree in the parlor. And in recent years, General Wayne had been a guest at our table.

Gone, all gone. Outside the schooner, the snow fell, thicker and thicker. Mama allowed me to have coffee with cream in it. She allowed me to have a second piece of cake for dessert. And she let little Louisa suck her thumb, without scolding.

I thought of Nat again up in Hartford, there to "grow up away from rivers and iron forges and cutting machines and the like, so he could grow up whole."

And I thought, *Mama, he isn't whole. None of us is. And it isn't rivers and iron forges and cutting machines that have done it to us. You have done much of it, Mama. You. But you still have a chance to keep us from being cut into little pieces. Oh, Mama, please. If only you could know it.*

But she did not. And I was afraid that she would never, no matter what.

CHAPTER TWENTY-EIGHT

M AMA'S REPUTATION took a turn for the worse.
In the spring of '89, right after General Washington was sworn in as our first president, in New York City, a man by the name of Jack Webb was going about the streets of Savannah saying spurious things about Mama, telling everyone he knew about her "unsavory activities."

None other than Phineas Miller accosted him. He caned him unmercifully on the street. It was in the *Savannah Republican,* the whole story, including how Miller had challenged Webb to a duel. Webb refused.

General Wayne came to the house, furious at Miller for creating such a fuss, for bringing the matter to public attention.

"It makes you look like a hero, yes," General Wayne told Miller. "I knew Webb in the army. He's an idiot and everybody knows it. Nobody would have paid mind to him. The whole business would have gone away on its own. But now the whole of Savannah—no, the *East*—is talking about Caty. Have you no sense, man?"

I sat on a nearby window seat, listening. Mama was in a chair, crying quietly.

"I never thought about it that way," Miller said.

"You don't think about a lot of things," Wayne chided.

Miller left the house. General Wayne stayed for supper. It was, for him, a temporary victory.

You would think Mama would be grateful to General Wayne for showing up as he did to comfort her, for bawling out Miller, for always being there when he was needed.

But for some reason she was growing more and more distant from him.

Perhaps it was because more and more bills were coming in.

Oh, bills were always coming in. She was accustomed to them by now. But bills from this particular creditor hurt her to the quick. And every time she received one from him, she took to her room for the day and cried.

Wadsworth.

He was sending her bills for debts Pa owed to him. Her old friend. Her lover.

"I distrust men more and more," she said to me one day when she received another bill from him. "I confess, he knows how these missives hurt me. He does not need the money. He does this just to injure my feelings."

But somehow she came up with the money to pay Wadsworth.

She sold the carriage, Pa's "extravaganza," the vehicle I had hidden in that day to go to the docks of Savannah to catch Eulinda before she boarded her ship. And with the proceeds, she paid Wadsworth.

"I will be beholden to no man," she told me.

Did that mean General Wayne? Is that why she drew away from him?

But GENERAL WAYNE still had the misfortune to love her in the spring of 1790.

I was a young woman now. A dancing master came once a week to the house to instruct me. He was a Frenchman of aristocratic background, of the planter class, by the name of the Marquis de Montalet. He lived on a nearby Savannah River plantation.

His wife had died, and after only two visits, he was in love with Mama. But he was content to only gaze at her from a distance.

He polished up my French, along with teaching me dancing.

As a young woman I could observe, more distinctly, that General Wayne was still in love with Mama. And that he still wanted to do things for her, to win her love over all the others.

When he visited, he often took walks with me. He confided in me like a grownup now.

His plantation was failing, he told me. He was going to run for national Congress as a representative from the Forty-first District from Georgia.

"If I make it, I can help your mother with her appeal," he told me.

My heart broke for him.

I had come upon a letter he had written to her, which she had left upon her ladies' desk in the front parlor. Mama had let me see it.

I pledge the honor of a soldier, it said, *that I will repay you with compound interest upon your personal demand, in any Quarter of the Globe.*

He was not talking about money. Mama had gone to New England at the time. And his grief was not to be borne at their parting.

He had known her for so many years—did he still not understand the depth of her cruelty? What did Mama have to do to prove it to him?

SHE DID IT in the spring of 1790 when she took another trip north with me and Louisa. As we were readying for the trip, I realized that we had not seen General Wayne for at least a week, that he did not know we were going.

"He'll likely be around," I reminded her. "Aren't you going to leave word for him? Say goodbye?"

"I owe him nothing," she told me. There was bitterness in the words.

I stopped what I was doing, which was helping her pack. We were in her room. I looked at her. "Mama?" I asked.

"And I owe you no explanation," she snapped.

"I wasn't asking for one," I flung back at her. But I had been and she knew it.

She threw to the floor some gloves she had in her hand. She sat on the bed she'd once shared with Pa.

"Oh, Cornelia, I know you like him. And he favors you. But all these years I have been patient and sympathized with him because he was estranged from his wife. I understood his need to seek out all his sweethearts. He is a man. I understood his needs, Lord knows. Even his on-again-off-again romance with Mary Maxwell and other girls in Savannah. None of it was serious. I knew that."

She paused, bowed her head. "And heaven knows, he put up with my transgressions. But now, for some reason, Cornelia, I can no longer put up with his."

I said nothing. I wanted to ask her if she loved him, but I did not dare.

I wanted, more than I wanted to breathe at the moment, to ask her if he was my father. Because the thought, the question, never left my mind. Never, over the past few years, did I ever stop thinking of it. Never did I stop wondering or hoping to find out.

But I understood what General Wayne wanted me to know.

That if I knew the truth, that if he was and I knew it,

I would never again think good of my mama. And he did not want that.

So there he was, protecting her again.

And if he was not my father, then nobody lost anything. But he would not tell me that he was not, either. He would not give me that. I had to earn that myself, he'd told me. I had to learn to love and trust the people concerned enough to believe it was not so.

But after what Mama had shown me over the past few years, I could not summon the love and trust for her. I just could not do it.

So there was General Wayne. And there was always the possibility that he could be my father. And I must live with it.

"I still think," I told Mama, "that you should have told him goodbye."

Because, I added to myself, *all you are doing is hurting him. Going out of your way to hurt him. And we only do that to people we love.*

After all, I was a young woman now. And as a young woman you know such things.

CHAPTER TWENTY-NINE

G ENERAL WAYNE was elected to Congress in 1791.
"Has Wayne gone?" Mama asked me.

"Yes, Mama."

He'd left half an hour ago, driven to Savannah by his man, Joshua, on his way to Philadelphia, the new seat of government.

He'd come to bid Mama goodbye. They were on good terms again, though not as good as before, never quite as good as before.

I'd listened while he'd told her how he'd severely bawled out his son, Isaac, for not continuing on with his education. Isaac was twenty, and Wayne was bitterly disappointed with him. And I thought, *I never want him to be that disappointed in me.*

He'd picked up little Louisa, who was seven now, and whirled her around and kissed her, then came over to me. He stood me in front of him, took my measure solemnly. "You are growing up," he accused.

"Yes, sir," I said.

He scowled his disapproval. "You weren't supposed to grow up," he said, "and you are too pretty by half. Does your mama allow you to associate with young men?"

Then, not waiting for my answer, he looked at her. "Caty?" he asked.

"She goes to dances, properly chaperoned," she told him.

He nodded solemnly. "Behave yourself," he admonished. "Don't disappoint me." He kissed my forehead.

I went outside to watch him leave. I waved him off.

When I returned to the house, Mama was sleeping on the settee. I let her sleep for a while, and when she woke, she asked me if he'd gone.

IN THE MONTHS that followed, Mama received letters from Wayne in Philadelphia. He had initiated a resolution on her behalf about her claim. He had secured votes in her favor, and then, by spring, she heard there was a movement in Georgia to unseat Wayne in Congress.

In mid-March, a vote was passed and he was unseated, and Mama lost one of her best friends in the House of Representatives.

Wayne came home to Georgia, and we did not see him for weeks.

There were rumors that he did not go out of his house, that he did not work his plantation, or go to the post office for his mail, that he was not paying his bills or his taxes.

"Mama," I begged, "we should go and see him. Assure ourselves that he is all right."

She said no. She was not angry with him, she promised me. She just did not wish to see him at the moment.

"Let me go, then," I begged.

"I absolutely forbid it!" she said. "A young girl does not go calling on a man alone. I absolutely forbid it!"

I worried for General Wayne. I worried for Mama, for she took to her room and cried.

It rained and it rained that spring. The rain pinged off the windows and splashed into the river ominously.

Because Mama was served her meals in her room, Louisa and I had to eat at the table with Phineas Miller, which meant we had to be courteous to him and keep up a conversation. After all, he was still the manager of the plantation, and he still tutored little Louisa on the side.

I received a letter from my brother George in France, the only thing that kept me sane during this time. He wrote that he was in "good health and spirits and as saucy as he pleased." He had, as I knew, been a guest at the Lafayette home on the Rue de Bourbon, but now, he wrote, he was with Lafayette's son, George Washington, in a boarding school run by Monsieur Frestel.

"Here, Madame Lafayette would pay us a daily visit," he said, "but no longer can, since a revolution has erupted and crazed mobs are out in the streets. Don't tell Mama. She will fret."

Crazed mobs in the streets?

I knew there were no crazed mobs between our plantation and that of Anthony Wayne's. I knew Mama was going, in two days, to Philadelphia, to see to her claim before Congress.

What else did I need to know?

CHAPTER THIRTY

AFTER MAMA WENT away again to Philadelphia, I left a note for Phineas Miller, saying that I was going to a friend's for the day. At least he could not complain to Mama that I went off without telling him, leaving him in a state of anxiety without knowing what had happened to me.

Then I went to the kitchen and asked Alexis for some fresh-baked bread to take with me. She wrapped up two loaves, then gave me a third—some gingerbread— awarding me with a secret smile when she handed it to me.

But she said nothing, asked no questions.

Did she know I was going to see General Wayne?

If she did, she would not tell. She had always liked Wayne, making his favorite dishes when he came, making sure he got extra-special portions of everything.

When I arrived at the Wayne plantation just before noon, the place seemed eerily quiet, almost deserted. And then I saw the peacocks on the lawn and the horses in the pasture. But only three of them, instead of a dozen. Had he sold the others off?

When I dismounted my horse by the barn and handed

him over to Joshua, he said yes, the general was home and I was to go right inside.

In the kitchen, Lila grinned when she welcomed me. "Good, company. Jus' what that man needs. Go right on in, chile. I'll make fresh coffee. Don't be taken 'back by how he looks. He jus' bein' careless 'bout himself these days."

It was what Mama would call an understatement.

General Wayne was slouched in a chair in front of the hearth. His head was resting in one hand. He was un-shaven, with about two days' worth of beard. His shirt was open at the collar. His boots were unpolished.

At his feet were three of his dogs. On top of his chair was his cat.

On a small table beside him was an empty cup of what had likely been coffee. Beside it was a small bottle of liquor.

The dogs roused themselves when I came into the room, growling threateningly.

The general came awake in an instant, drew himself to his feet, saw me, and quieted the dogs. "Hush." And when they did not hush, he spoke sternly. "Quiet," he said. "Down!"

They obeyed. *Anybody would obey that voice,* I thought.

He drew himself up tall, like the soldier he was. "Cornelia," he said. "Come in, child. Is everything all right at home?"

"Yes, sir," I went into the room and sat in the chair where he gestured I should sit.

He became aware of his appearance of a sudden, ran his hand through his hair, then over his face, and then looked sheepish. "I'm sorry. I'm a mess. I don't like you seeing me like this. I represent the perfect opposite of the discipline that is instilled in every soldier."

"It's all right, General Wayne. You have a right to look however you like in your own house."

He appeared surprised at my answer. "You are quite grown up. And understanding," he said. "You are going to be quite a woman someday, Cornelia."

Lila came in then with fresh coffee, fruit, and the gingerbread. He smiled, seeing the gingerbread. "I'm surprised your mother let you ride over alone," he told me.

"She didn't. Mama's gone to Philadelphia. If she knew I'd even come to call on you, she'd be furious. She forbade me to come. Much less alone."

"Is that so? And why is that?"

"Because," I said bravely, "we heard how you were living." And I told him about the rumors.

He said nothing for a moment. Just stirred his coffee meditatively. "The rumors are true," he admitted. "I've been morose and melancholy, and I've hidden away from the rest of the world. My conduct has been shabby. My spirits have been on the ground. I've been an unhappy man, Cornelia."

Tears came to my eyes and, by sheer willpower that I had never been able to summon before, I refused to let them overflow. "I'm sorry, General Wayne," I told him.

"If my son acted in such a manner, I'd shake some

sense into him until he came 'round," he said. "Then I'd slap his face, just for good measure. But I can do nothing for myself."

I offered nothing. I just listened, for it was all I could do.

"It isn't just my being unseated in Congress that's rendered me this way," he confessed, "though that was a blow." He lowered his head. "James Jackson, who lost to me in the election, led the impeachment proceedings. He convinced the others that my election was a fraud."

He looked up and smiled at me sadly. "Your father always hated politics. I should have followed his way of thinking. But no, Cornelia, it isn't just that. Something else put me into the doldrums."

I came alert.

"Child," he said, "I found out in the county courthouse in Savannah that your mother and Phineas Miller have recorded a legal agreement concerning a prospective marriage."

I just stared at him for a moment. "They are getting married?" I knew I sounded like the village idiot.

He nodded yes.

"Sometime in the future, not now. The document says that Miller disclaims any property from the Greene estate. Your mother can't get married now. Her status as a widow is most important in her petition to Congress.

"And," he added, "to me. Just knowing of that document was enough to push me over the edge."

"When do you think they will wed?" I asked.

"Knowing your mother, I'd say not for a while yet, not even if her petition is agreed upon by Congress. Women become the property of their husbands once they wed, Cornelia. Your mother is not likely, anytime soon, to hand herself over to be anybody's property.

"A woman has to hand her children over to her husband, to be held under his jurisdiction. Once wed, women can't take part in any court action, keep any earnings. God, *they have no rights!* So I wouldn't worry about it. Not just yet."

"But you admit, you've got the miseries over it."

He scowled. "She's signed a marriage agreement with him, Cornelia. Our relations are finished."

He shrugged. "One good thing has come out of my miseries, though," he confided. "My son and daughter, having heard of my state, have both written to me. And I haven't heard from either of them in quite a while. Their letters were very endearing."

"I'm glad, sir."

He nodded. "You shouldn't have come here alone," he chided, giving the conversation a turn. "If your mother finds out . . ." He shook his head sorrowfully.

"She won't, sir. You won't tell her, will you?"

"I'd only have to whip you again."

We both laughed about that and his eyes found mine, warmly.

"Well, anyway, I've laid the groundwork in the House

for your mother to get approval for her claim. The roll call vote should be taken this week. She has friends who will favor her."

"I thank you for what you did for her before you left, sir."

He nodded.

"What will you do now?"

"Now? I will loaf about. I will do nothing."

"You can't do that," I said.

"Oh? And why can't I? Where does a young snip of a girl get the right to tell me what I am to do with the rest of my life?"

He looked at me hard, with those hazel eyes, as if to say, *Even if she is my daughter.*

I blushed and looked down. "Because you are a hero of the Revolution to everyone, sir. And all look up to you."

The muscles in his jaw set. His face sobered. "You are right," he said. "I have a name to live up to, even if I am not that person people think I am."

He stood up, rubbing his beard, walked to the window that overlooked the lawn, and thought for a moment. "How is your brother George?" he asked of a sudden.

"I just had a letter from him." I told him of the news, of what was going on in France, the mobs in the streets and everything.

"Yes, yes," he murmured. "I've read of it. You know, Cornelia, we've exported cotton in this country—tobacco, rice, lumber, so much. But do you know what our first significant export is?"

"No, sir."

"Revolution," he said.

"I never thought of it that way, sir."

"You should. Everybody should. Still. Your mother should bring George home soon." He walked back and forth, ruminating. He sighed heavily.

"We're going to have war again, soon. In the old northwest. The Indians are being badly mishandled out there right now. First by General Harman and now by St. Clair. The army they have is small and unfit. A new army is going to be thrown together."

He did not have to say any more to me. I understood. He just smiled.

But I felt a stab, as if someone had bayoneted me inside.

I forced a smile back. He was still a soldier, after all.

"It's what I would need to bring me back to life again," he said. "And I have to get away from here. I can't stay within a hundred—no, a *thousand*—miles of your mother if she marries that idiot. Or I'll die a slow and agonizing death, as if I were tied to the ground and being devoured by hundreds of thousands of man-eating ants. Of course, I'll have to get a commission, if President Washington would be so kind as to give it to me."

I knew I should not say what I was about to say.

But I also knew two things. One, that he *would* die if he stayed.

And, two, that I loved him too much to see it happen. Be he my father or not.

No, chances were that I would never know if he was my father. But that did not matter anymore.

In my heart, somewhere in some small corner, he would always be my father. And if there was the slightest chance of it, I would not leave him here to die.

"Sir," I said, "mayhap Mama could put in a good word with President Washington for you. He and Mrs. Washington like her considerable much. And they can't say enough good things about Pa."

He looked grave. "Let's wait and see if your mother gets the money she's petitioned Congress for, first," he said.

Then he brightened. "Tell you what," he said. "You give me an hour. That's all I need to shave and clean up. Browse among my books here. Romp outside with the dogs. Talk with Lila in the kitchen. When I look human again, I'll ride with you home."

"I can't let Phineas Miller see you, or know I've been here, sir."

"We'll part a short distance from the house," he promised. "As a gentleman of honor, I cannot let you ride home alone."

CHAPTER THIRTY-ONE

MAMA RECEIVED her compensation from Congress for all the money of Pa's that he had given out to sustain his troops during the war.

President Washington himself signed the bill.

Mama came home that spring, bubbling with joy. All her money worries were over. Congress had given her the first installment of forty-seven thousand dollars.

Alexander Hamilton himself signed the check.

Mama was a different woman. She spoke about bringing Nat and George and Martha home. She talked about a party.

"How sweet is justice," she said. "I feel as saucy as you please."

She did have a party, and she invited General Wayne. He came, garbed spotlessly, mingling among the guests, behaving as if he never knew there was a legal agreement that bespoke marriage between Mama and Phineas Miller in the county courthouse in Savannah.

Only I saw the pained look on his face when he was standing to the side on one occasion, observing Mama and Phineas dancing.

He left the party early, claiming one of his mares had

been starting to give birth when he left. He bowed to Mama and kissed her hand upon leaving.

"MAMA, PLEASE," I begged her, "you must do this, please."

"There is nothing I *must* do, Cornelia. And I do not appreciate you speaking to me like that."

"I am sorry, Mama. But you yourself said that you and we children would have been objects of charity if General Wayne had not kept his seat in Congress long enough to do you such essential services. That it was to his exertions that you owe your independence. Did you not, Mama? Did you not say that?"

"And what if I did, Cornelia? Are you saying I am now beholden to him? You know I do not like to be beholden to any man."

"Mama, I never said you were beholden. General Wayne is the last person in the world who would want you to be."

"So, then, let the matter lie fallow."

"Mama, you can't! He needs a good word put in with the president for him! That's all he needs. And you can do it. You know how President Washington likes you."

"What, bother President Washington with a request so soon again? My dear Cornelia, you should learn now to save your requests to a man for important matters. And make them few and far between, lest the man tire of you."

"Mama, this is important! General Wayne has nothing now! His plantation is failing. He's been put out of Congress. And . . ."

"And what?" she asked.

Oh, how I longed to tell her that I knew of her agreement with Phineas Miller. That Wayne knew of it and that it was killing him. But I could not. For I had promised the general that I would never let on to Mama that we knew of her plans to wed Miller.

My hands, my tongue, and my heart were tied.

I sighed and turned away, tears coming to my eyes.

But Mama discerned my distress. "What is it, Cornelia? Why are you so concerned about General Wayne?" Her voice had softened.

I bit my bottom lip before answering. I said what I could say. "I observed his face at the party you had, Mama. When you were dancing with Mr. Miller."

"And?"

"He still loves you, Mama."

She looked down at the magazine. "I never did more than flirt with him, Cornelia. Women always have the right to flirt, if it is kept a harmless pastime. Men expect it from us. If we do it properly, it gives us power, and Lord knows we have little of that. But we must learn to do it properly. It's about time you learned how, don't you think?"

I just stared at her. I did not answer. *Is that what she calls what she'd been doing with Phineas Miller the day I caught her in the schoolroom with him, so long ago now? And what she'd done with all the others? Even General Wayne? Is that what she dismisses it all as now? Flirting?*

"I do not wish to do this thing, Cornelia. If I ask the president this favor, he will grant it. And then Wayne will go far away."

Something fell inside me, smashed into bits on the floor of my soul. *She still loves him, too! And she wants him around! Though she might wed Miller, she cannot bear to let Wayne go! She would rather keep him on a line, like a fish, and watch him struggle and suffer! What kind of love is that?*

"Mama," I begged, weakly now. "Please, if President Washington will grant your favor, please ask it. In Pa's name. Please."

Then I left the room.

GENERAL ANTHONY WAYNE put in for a commission with the president of the United States. He did not know that I had asked Mama to write to George Washington. I did not tell him. If Mama ever did, I do not know.

I only know that he not only received his commission from the president, but was named commander in chief of the army.

He was to go west with the army, to the frontier, to the region of the Great Lakes.

Congress gave him much power and many advantages. They told him that they knew he would conduct a well-administered, well-planned, and well-executed campaign.

They knew he would finally bring peace to the frontier.

He came to see us before he left.

Nat and Martha were home by then, for it was now well into 1792. Mama had not yet married Phineas Miller. I was older now and in possession of a knowledge that weighed on me like a suit of armor.

I knew things inside my soul that often made tears appear for no reason at all, things no daughter should be conscious of, things my sister Martha had yet no inkling of.

We had a special dinner in honor of General Wayne's departure.

Phineas Miller was not present at the table. The fault was mine.

At the cost of my well-being, my good standing with Mama, I had gone to him in the stable the day before and spoken to him.

In the king's English I told him plain that General Wayne was coming to sup the next day to say goodbye. That he was going away for years.

Mayhap for good. That we might never see him again.

There were tears in my voice when I told him this, and I did not try to dispense with them.

"He and my mama have been friends since the old days," I said, "since the war. Since Mama was first married to Pa. Since Valley Forge. It was because of his exertions in Congress that she had her petition answered. Or she, and we children, would be beggars now. She has—how shall I say it?—feelings of delicacy for him. Do you understand, Mr. Miller?"

He said yes, he quite understood.

I said, "Good, then you will also understand why I would be beholden to you if tomorrow evening you told Mama that you almost forgot, but of a sudden you remembered that you had a previous engagement and could not make the dinner appointment. Could you do that? Not for me, Mr. Miller. There is no reason on God's good earth why you should do anything for me. But for my mama. Would you do it for my mama? So she could have one last evening with General Wayne. Remember, they may never see each other again. He is going off to the frontier, to try to tame the wild Indians. Wild Indians aren't easy to tame, you know."

He said yes, he would do it.

I forgave him for everything then. I don't know what I would have done if he'd said no. Likely picked up a shovel and knocked him over the head and rendered him unconscious so he wouldn't be able to come to the supper, anyway.

THE DINNER WAS OVER. Outside it was twilight. Somehow I had managed to get Martha and Nat and Louisa away from the table so Mama and General Wayne could linger alone over their coffee.

The March air was soft and warm and in the west the sky still held the red and orange streaks of a leftover sunset. And leftover dreams.

"I think," I proposed to my sisters and brother, "that we ought to go upstairs and leave them to themselves to say goodbye."

I had summoned the strength of the eldest. Martha, having been under the thumbs of the nuns for so long, had become submissive and was no longer threatening.

I, on the other hand, had learned what I must, being so exposed to life here, living under nobody's thumb, not even Mama's. I had learned to be obstinate, persistent, stubborn, self-reliant, and cagey.

The others complied. We went upstairs to our separate rooms.

About nine, according to the grandfather clock in the downstairs hall, we were summonded by Emily.

General Wayne wanted to bid us goodbye.

I went downstairs and watched as the others dutifully said goodbye. They hugged him while I stood aside. They tendered their best wishes, promised to be good, wished him well. Mama was nowhere to be seen. They went up to bed. I hung back in the corner, in the shadows in the front hall.

He started to walk to the front door, and with his back to me, gestured with his arm that I should follow.

I went with him, out onto the front veranda.

We stood there a moment. Priam was bringing around his horse.

"Well, then," Wayne said to me.

"Yes, sir."

"I want to thank you."

"For what, sir?"

In the near dark, broken only by torches in huge iron sconces in the ground, he took my hand. "For whatever you did to get Miller out of the way tonight. And for getting your mother to petition the president for me."

"Sir, I didn't—"

"Shhh. I am the one who taught you to lie, remember. I know lies when I hear them. I know your mother wouldn't have done such on her own, that she wanted me around. I know you wanted me around, too, Cornelia. Real love is courage. Thank you."

I wanted to flee. I was going to cry.

He put a hand on my shoulder. Then he touched the side of my face. "I don't know when we'll see each other again, Cornelia, but I want you to know some things."

I took a deep breath. *Is he going to tell me now that he is my father?*

No, I decided. *Because he's said that real love is courage, that's why.*

"You may marry before we see each other again. Be careful in that direction. Remember what I told you of the rights women lose when they wed. That doesn't mean you should not wed. There is no more beautiful thing than a good marriage. Just make sure you pick the right one."

"Yes, sir."

"Write to me, if you wish, and tell me about him. Letters do find their way, you know."

"Yes, sir."

His hand had reached my hair now. He was fondling a strand of it, tucking it behind my ear. "And always guard your honor, Cornelia. I tell you this like a father. The man you choose must respect you."

I nodded. *Like a father!*

But he would never tell. He would face the most savage Indian before he would tell me. He would not allow me to disrespect my mother because of something they might have done a long time ago.

If it was true, he would not allow me to change my allegiances from my pa to him.

And if it were not true, well mayhap, just mayhap, he wanted me to believe, in a small corner of my heart, that there was the remotest possibility that he was my father.

He would never, never tell.

And now, standing there before him in the near dark, I knew that I did not want him to.

"Goodbye, Cornelia," he said.

"Goodbye, General Wayne."

We hugged. He held me close. The hug said all kinds of things we could never say to each other. And the best part about that hug was that we both knew it, when he turned and mounted his horse and rode off into the night.

EPILOGUE

I NEVER SAW General Wayne again.

I did write to him a few times, and he to me. I received a letter from him from Pittsburgh, where he was training his troops. It was in the fall of '92 and he seemed very vigorous and happy.

I wrote him of the arrival, at Mulberry Grove, of a man named Eli Whitney, another Yale graduate, whom Mama had met aboard ship on the way home from New York with Miller. Whitney had been coming to Savannah to teach, but became sick, and Mama invited him to Mulberry Grove to recuperate. I wrote how he and Mama and Miller went on home, and I stayed on the winter in Philadelphia with the Washingtons. And the president asked after him.

And how, when I got back home in the spring, Whitney was still there at Mulberry Grove and toying with an invention he had in mind.

Something he called a cotton gin. He and Miller spent hours poring over it.

I told him Miller and Mama were still not yet wed.

He wrote back that he was going on north and was naming a place in Ohio Greenville, in honor of Pa.

By the next year, I received another letter from a place called Fort Defiance. The battered and spattered envelope had taken three months to get to me. He said Fort Defiance was at the junction of the Maumee and Anglaise rivers, north of this place called Greenville. The Indians had refused his offer of peace. And he was going to meet them.

I said I would pray for him. I told him that we were all together again at Mulberry Grove, that George had finally arrived home, that he was strong and well educated and sent his best hopes and wished he could be with him.

Wayne wrote that I might not hear from him for a while and not to worry if I didn't. And if I had another letter, to send it on to this same address, as it would, sooner or later, find him.

I did have another letter.

I sent it to him that spring of '94, only a few weeks after George returned home.

George had invited a friend named Stits to stay the summer, I wrote. And he and Stits had launched a canoe in the river. They were going in the canoe all the way to Savannah. The river was swollen from the spring rains, and about an hour after they left, Stits came back, scarce able to walk, muddy and ashen-faced. The canoe had overturned. He had barely been able to get himself above water, then could not find either George or the canoe. He walked on the muddy shore back to us. All of the household, I reported to Wayne, went out to search for George. We went in boats, in the direction in which the boys had gone. We searched the rest of the day and half the night. No George.

Then, at dawn, my brother's limp body washed ashore in front of Mulberry Grove. Mama was unable to be consoled, I told him. *And oh, how we needed you. Only you could have consoled her. And I know, sir, that even as I write this I am unfair to do so.*

In a return letter, he said he had written to Mama to console her, best as he could. And to me he sent his most profound sympathies for the loss of my brother, who "would most likely have turned out to be as good a man as your pa. I mourn his untimely passing, which is nothing less than a tragedy."

He was in a place called Fallen Timbers, he said, a place the Indians called "the sharp ends of the guns." It was where they broke and ran before his army. "We hope," he wrote, "for surrender within the year in Greenville."

Just about this time, the first cotton gins, invented successfully by Eli Whitney and manufactured in New Haven, came to Savannah. These gins, run by one man and a horse, cleaned cotton so much better than the older machines that took the labor of fifty men. The invention was turning the South upside down. Visitors by the score were coming to our plantation.

Northern industrialists were sending representatives to investigate the possibilities.

One such was a young man named John Nightengale. He was twenty-four and an heir of a prominent New

England family. And the possibility he saw was in my sister Martha.

They were married in the spring of 1795 at Mulberry Grove.

Right after that, General Wayne wrote to me that the Indians had surrendered to him at Greenville, Ohio. I thought how fitting that they should do it there, in the place he had named for Pa.

There was a scrawled postscript to the letter. *The truth of the matter you so dearly need, my dear Cornelia, is that I really don't know. Out here in the wilderness I have decided that I owe you the truth, that you are old enough to take it. And that is all the truth I can give. Forgive me.*

I clutched the letter to my breast while tears ran down my face. *Dear man. Oh, you dear man, thank you.*

I wrote back to him immediately. I congratulated him on his victory. And then I included a postscript that said, simply, *Thank you and God bless you always. There is nothing to forgive. You have given me much. Love, Cornelia.*

Mama wed Phineas Miller on the last day of May in 1796. I did not write to Wayne to tell him. I am glad I did not tell him. And I am glad I sent a letter back to him immediately after he wrote to me. I received a last note from him from Detroit, in November.

It said, briefly, *Thank you, dear girl, thank you for your forgiveness.* That was all.

General Wayne died on the fifteenth of December of

1796 in Erie, Pennsylvania, on his way home from occupying Detroit.

Mama cried when she found out. I cried with her. And I never told her what Wayne had finally told me.

In April 1801, I married a man named Peyton Skipwith Jr. I was twenty-four. All I will say is that although he was from a leading family from Virginia, he was no pantywaist. He reminded me a lot of Wayne. I followed General Wayne's instructions as to a husband, and I know Wayne would have approved.

In 1803, Dungeness, the home Pa so wanted on Cumberland Island, was finally finished. It was built just as Pa wanted it. And the room on the fourth floor was there.

My sister Martha never claimed that room. Peyton and I stayed in it when we visited.

And every time we visited, I looked for that horse I had seen that day, a lifetime ago now. Several times I thought I saw it, but when I ran to find it, it was gone.

It was as if I were running after a dream. Like I had so often run after the truth of General Wayne being my father.

And now there was always the possibility that he was.

And what was I to do now with that possibility?

Just smile sometimes to myself, and nourish it.

For it is possible, then, that I have had two fathers. Both wonderful. Twice the love. And twice the loss. For I have lost both.

AUTHOR'S NOTE

Catharine Littlefield Greene, wife of Major General Nathanael Greene, has always been known as one of the most famous women of the American Revolution. She is listed right up there along with Martha Washington and Lucy Knox, wife of artillery officer Brigadier General Henry Knox, and other wives who spent the terrible winter of 1777–78 at Valley Forge.

When Caty Greene arrived at Valley Forge in February of 1778, she had left her two children with family in Rhode Island. She had not seen her beloved husband since the summer before. It was here that she met the Marquis de Lafayette, with whom she conversed in French, and the dashing young major general of the Continental Army Anthony Wayne.

It was the time of the French Alliance. There was a great celebration to honor the occasion. Caty Greene rode in the carriage with Martha Washington, who had taken her under her wing, and with whom she had become fast friends, as she had with many others in those trying times. Including General Wayne.

Reading about Caty Greene, often called Kitty, so enticed me that I was driven to go back to her childhood

and learn more. That childhood was even more rewarding. I found that she grew up on Block Island, off the
coast of New England, twelve miles off Rhode Island.
There was, we are told, "a sense of timelessness on the
isle." And Caty's life, as a child of a family of means, was
sheltered and secluded. She ran free. Her father was "a
distinguished man, a deputy to the General Assembly, a
man of love, warmth, and fun, who liked to cuddle little
children in his lap and tell them stories," according to the
book *Caty: A Biography of Catharine Littlefield Greene,*
which I mention in my bibliography.

Her mother died when she was ten, and shortly after,
she was sent to live with Aunt Catharine Greene, in East
Greenwich, Rhode Island.

Caty Littlefield, as she was then, grew in character for
me, as is necessary for a personage to do to become a pro-
tagonist in my book.

"But what will you do to satisfy my readers?" I
asked her.

"You just wait and see," she promised. "You don't
know anything about me yet."

Well, I waited. Soon she met young Nathanael Greene,
from a good Quaker family, but himself a Quaker no
more, for he had other fish to fry. He was near six feet tall,
with a firm jaw, with fire in his soul for the Whig cause,
yet with clear, quiet eyes and a gentle manner. She introduced me to him. After I got to know Nathanael and his
family, she convinced me that she should marry him, despite the difference in their ages.

He was all of twelve years older than she was.

Well, that was something worth sitting up and taking notice of, I supposed.

When she came of age, they wed. Caty Greene was beautiful, lively of spirit, spritely, and gay. And she and Nathanael were wed only a short time when the war came.

So THEN, my readers, you ask, is it all true, everything in the book? Did it all really happen that way?

Let me remind you, dear readers, that this is a work of *historical fiction*, which means I am fictionalizing what really did happen. Yes, Caty Littlefield really did grow up on Block Island, her mother did die when she was ten, she was sent to live with Aunt Catharine, she did meet Nathanael Greene, and he was twelve years older than she, all as I have written. But those are the *facts!* It is up to the writer to fill in the story, to tell how they imagine it happened.

And so I did, with part 1.

But then what about part 2?

I wanted to take the book further along. To tell the story of Cornelia, Caty's daughter, to tell of Caty's family.

When I read of how Caty's Aunt Catharine had supposedly had an affair with Benjamin Franklin and it caused so much gossip, of how beautiful Caty herself was, of how her enticing moods and her gaiety kept the men's spirits up at Valley Forge, I likened her to Aunt Catharine. And then I read of Caty's friendships, later in life, with other men, even after she was married to Nathanael. And I read how General Wayne kept coming around to visit her and Nathanael at their plantation in Georgia, a fact that generated more gossip, and I decided to make this all very uncomfortable for her daughter Cornelia.

And so I made the focus of the second part of the book the rumor that General Wayne is Cornelia's father, because she was conceived at Valley Forge and because she, Cornelia, is the only one who has hazel eyes, as has General Wayne.

Her sister Martha, who constantly vies with Cornelia for their father's love, plants this thought in Cornelia's mind to drive her crazy. And so the tension in the second part of the book takes off from there.

None of this really happened in the family of Nathanael Greene. It is pure fiction, and this great and good man had no part in it. It was put in for the sake of story. Of course, he always knew his wife was a flirt, but he put up with it, and as far as anyone knows they had a good marriage. As I say, I did it for the sake of story. It is well known, however, that General Anthony Wayne, hero of the American Revolution, a very real hero, was a ladies' man, and that there were real feelings between him and Caty Greene. I took it upon myself as a writer of fiction to take the whole thing a little further. General Wayne respected and admired his friend General Greene too much to dishonor that friendship in any way.

It is true that Caty's son George did drown in the river, and the manner of Nathanael's death is also true. Her marriage to Phineas Miller is fact, also. In defense of Caty Greene, women did not have it easy in that era. Their presence in the home, their behavior and labor were most important to the survival of their family. They were totally dependent upon their husband, his demands, those of the family, and the social strictures. If they married well and the man was "of good parts," they could be happy. If they married poor or if their husband was mean, they were destined to be miserable. In either case their fate was to have many children, and the wear and tear on their bodies could, and often did, kill them.

As General Wayne told Cornelia in the book: "During the war, the social rules were relaxed, and at Valley Forge we did as we pleased and had a good time. After the war, we expected the same thing. But found that out in the world, nothing had changed. That kiss I gave your mother meant nothing. It was just something like we used to do at Valley Forge."

Was it? It was something that Cornelia, and my reader, must figure out for themselves.

Ann Rinaldi

BIBLIOGRAPHY

Berkin, Carol. *Revolutionary Mothers: Women in the Struggle for America's Independence.* New York: Alfred A. Knopf, 2005.

Boatner, Mark Mayo, III. *Encyclopedia of the American Revolution.* New York: David McKay Company, 1966.

Carbone, Gerald M. *Nathanael Greene: A Biography of the American Revolution.* New York: Palgrave Macmillan, 2008.

Langguth, A. J. *Patriots: The Men Who Started the American Revolution.* New York: Simon and Schuster, 1988.

Showman, Richard K. *The Papers of Nathanael Greene, vol. 2* (1 January 1777–16 October 1778). Chapel Hill, N.C.: Rhode Island Historical Society, 1980.

Spruill, Juila Cherry. *Women's Life and Work in the Southern Colonies.* Chapel Hill: University of North Carolina Press, 1972. Published simultaneously in Canada by George J. McLeod Limited, Toronto, copyright 1972 by W.W. Norton & Co. Inc.

Stegeman, John F., and Janet A. Stegeman. *Caty: A Biography of Catharine Littlefield Greene.* Athens: University of Georgia Press, 1977.

Tagney, Ronald N. *The World Turned Upside Down.* West Newbury, Mass.: Essex County History, 1989.